William Shakespeare's As You Like It: A Retelling in Prose

David Bruce

Published by David Bruce, 2022.

This is a work of fiction. Similarities to real people, places, or events are entirely coincidental.

WILLIAM SHAKESPEARE'S AS YOU LIKE IT: A RETELLING IN PROSE

First edition. July 22, 2022.

ISBN: 979-8201754372

Written by David Bruce.

Table of Contents

Dedication

Dedicated to Carl Eugene Bruce and Josephine Saturday Bruce

My father, Carl Eugene Bruce, died on 24 October 2013. He used to work for Ohio Power, and at one time, his job was to shut off the electricity of people who had not paid their bills. He sometimes would find a home with an impoverished mother and some children. Instead of shutting off their electricity, he would tell the mother that she needed to pay her bill or soon her electricity would be shut off. He would write on a form that no one was home when he stopped by because if no one was home he did not have to shut off their electricity.

The best good deed that anyone ever did for my father occurred after a storm that knocked down many power lines. He and other linemen worked long hours and got wet and cold. Their feet were freezing because water got into their boots and soaked their socks. Fortunately, a kind woman gave my father and the other linemen dry socks to wear.

My mother, Josephine Saturday Bruce, died on 14 June 2003. She used to work at a store that sold clothing. One day, an impoverished mother with a baby clothed in rags walked into the store and started shoplifting in an interesting way: The mother took the rags off her baby and dressed the infant in new clothing. My mother knew that this mother could not afford to buy the clothing, but she helped the mother dress her baby and then she watched as the mother walked out of the store without paying.

***

The doing of good deeds is important. As a free person, you can choose to live your life as a good person or as a bad person. To be a good person, do good deeds. To be a bad person, do bad deeds. If you do good deeds, you will become good. If you do bad deeds, you will become bad. To become the person you want to be, act as if you already are that kind of person. Each of us chooses what kind of person we will become. To become a good person, do the things a good person does. To become a bad person, do the things a bad person does. The opportunity to take action to become the kind of person you want to be is yours.

Human beings have free will. According to the Babylonian Niddah 16b, whenever a baby is to be conceived, the Lailah (angel in charge of contraception) takes the drop of semen that will result in the conception and asks God, “Sovereign of the Universe, what is going to be the fate of this drop? Will it develop into a robust or into a weak person? An intelligent or a stupid person? A wealthy or a poor person?” The Lailah asks all these questions, but it does not ask, “Will it develop into a righteous or a wicked person?” The answer to that question lies in the decisions to be freely made by the human being that is the result of the conception.

A Buddhist monk visiting a class wrote this on the chalkboard: “EVERYONE WANTS TO SAVE THE WORLD, BUT NO ONE WANTS TO HELP MOM DO THE DISHES.” The students laughed, but the monk then said, “Statistically, it’s highly unlikely that any of you will ever have the opportunity to run into a burning orphanage and rescue an infant. But, in the smallest gesture of kindness — a warm smile, holding the door for the person behind you, shoveling the driveway of the elderly person next door — you have committed an act of immeasurable profundity, because to each of us, our life is our universe.”

In her book titled *I Have Chosen to Stay and Fight*, comedian Margaret Cho writes, “I believe that we get complimentary snack-size portions of the afterlife, and we all receive them in a different way.” For Ms. Cho, many of her snack-size portions of the afterlife come in hip hop music. Other people get different snack-size portions of the afterlife, and we all must be on the lookout for them when they come our way. And perhaps doing good deeds and experiencing good deeds are snack-size portions of the afterlife.

The Zen master Gisan was taking a bath. The water was too hot, so he asked a student to add some cold water to the bath. The student brought a bucket of cold water, added some cold water to the bath, and then threw the rest of the water on a rocky path. Gisan scolded the student: “Everything can be used. Why did you waste the rest of the water by pouring it on the path? There are some plants nearby which could have used the water. What right do you have to waste even a drop of water?” The student became enlightened and changed his name to Tekisui, which means “Drop of Water.”

Cover Photograph for William Shakespeare's *As You Like It*: A Retelling in Prose:

Adina Voicu

https://pixabay.com/en/users/AdinaVoicu-485024/

https://pixabay.com/en/girl-princess-blond-hair-dress-724716/

Educate Yourself

Read Like A Wolf Eats

Be Excellent to Each Other

Books Then, Books Now, Books Forever

***

In this retelling, as in all my retellings, I have tried to make the work of literature accessible to modern readers who may lack some of the knowledge about mythology, religion, and history that the literary work's contemporary audience had.

Do you know a language other than English? If you do, I give you permission to translate this book, copyright your translation, publish or self-publish it, and keep all the royalties for yourself. (Do give me credit, of course, for the original retelling.)

I would like to see my retellings of classic literature used in schools, so I give permission to the country of Finland (and all other countries) to give copies of this book to all students forever. I also give permission to the state of Texas (and all other states) to give copies of this book to all students forever. I also give permission to all teachers to give copies of this book to all students forever.

Teachers need not actually teach my retellings. Teachers are welcome to give students copies of my eBooks as background material. For example, if they are teaching Homer's *Iliad* and *Odyssey*, teachers are welcome to give students copies of my *Virgil's* Aeneid: *A Retelling in Prose* and tell students, "Here's another ancient epic you may want to read in your spare time."

CAST OF CHARACTERS

DUKE SENIOR, living in exile.

FREDERICK, his Brother, Usurper of his Dominions.

AMIENS & JAQUES: Lords attending upon the banished Duke.

LE BEAU, a Courtier, attending upon Frederick.

CHARLES, a Wrestler.

OLIVER, JAQUES, & ORLANDO: Sons of Sir Rowland de Boys.

ADAM & DENNIS: Servants to Oliver.

TOUCHSTONE, a Clown.

SIR OLIVER MARTEXT, a Vicar.

CORIN & SILVIUS: Shepherds.

WILLIAM, a Country Fellow, in love with Audrey.

A person representing Hymen, god of marriage.

The Women

ROSALIND, Daughter to the banished Duke.

CELIA, Daughter to Frederick.

PHOEBE, a Shepherdess.

AUDREY, a Country Wench.

Other Characters

Lords, Pages, Foresters, and Attendants.

CHAPTER 1

— 1.1 —

Orlando, the third and youngest son of Sir Rowland de Boys, was talking about his life with Adam, an aged servant of the de Boys family. Some of Orlando's problems in life came from primogeniture, in which the bulk of the family estate is passed down to the oldest son, leaving much less of an inheritance for any younger sons. Such was the case with Orlando. The oldest son's name was Oliver, and Orlando and Adam were talking in Oliver's garden.

Orlando said, "I remember, Adam, that this is the reason why my father left me in his will the small sum of a thousand crowns. But as you said, he also gave my oldest brother, Oliver, the responsibility of raising me well — as a gentleman — if Oliver was to receive our father's blessing. Oliver is raising the middle brother — Jaques — well. Oliver sent him to the university, and according to all reports he is making wonderful progress. But Oliver keeps me at home like a person without money in rural areas. But is 'keep' the right word for a gentleman of my birth? My 'keep' is much like the keeping of an ox in a stall. Oliver's horses are better taken care of than I am. They are well fed, and well-paid hostlers teach them what they need to know. But I, his own brother, gain nothing under him but bodily growth into adulthood. Even the animals lying on dunghills to keep warm owe him that much. Besides this nothing that he so plentifully gives me, the something that nature gave me — my social standing by birth — his behavior seems to seek to take away from me. He lets me eat with his farm workers, will not allow me the place of a brother, and, as much as he is able to, he undermines my noble birth with a lack of proper education. Adam, this grieves me, and the spirit of my father, which I think is within me, begins to mutiny against this brother-imposed servitude. I will no longer endure it, though so far I know no intelligent way to avoid it."

Adam looked away and then replied, "Yonder comes my master, your eldest brother."

Orlando said, "Go stand aside, Adam, and you shall hear how he will taunt me."

Oliver walked up to Orlando and said mockingly, "Now, sir! What are you doing here?"

"Nothing," Orlando replied. "I can do nothing. I have not been educated to make anything of myself."

"If you are not making anything, then what are you marring?"

"Sir, I am helping you to mar that which God made, a poor unworthy brother of yours. I am marring myself with idleness for lack of something better to do."

"Then be better employed, and be quick about it."

"Shall I keep your hogs and eat scraps with them? That is what the prodigal son did in Luke 15:11-32. He received his inheritance and spent it and was forced to become a servant swineherd and eat the swine's food to keep himself from starving. But what prodigal portion have I spent, that I should come to such penury as did the prodigal son? I have never received my inheritance."

"Do you know where you are, sir?"

"Very well, sir. I am in your garden."

"Do you know to whom you are speaking, sir?"

"Yes, I know you better than you know me," Orlando replied. "I know that you are my eldest brother, and you should know that I share your heritage and family and blood. According to primogeniture, you are my better, because you were first born, but primogeniture does not deny my heritage. Even if twenty brothers were born in between you and me, I would still have as much of our father in me as you have. However, I confess that your being born first makes you the head of our family and therefore entitled to more respect than I am."

Angry, Oliver hit Orlando and called him a name: "Take that, boy!"

Angered by the blow and the insult, Orlando seized Oliver and held on to him to protect himself from any more blows.

He said to Oliver, "You are too young in strength; you are weaker than I am, and you are not the fighter that I am."

"Do you dare to lay hands on me, villain!"

A villain can be either a rogue or a peasant. Oliver used the word to mean "rogue," but in his reply Orlando used the other meaning.

"A villain is a peasant," Orlando said. "I am no villain. I am the youngest son of Sir Rowland de Boys; he was my father. Anyone who says that such a father gave birth to villains is three times a villain. If you were not my brother, I would not take this hand from your throat until my other hand had pulled out your tongue for saying that our father had given birth to a villain. By saying that, you have insulted yourself."

Adam said, "Sweet masters, don't fight. In memory of your father and for your father's sake, make peace with each other."

Oliver said, "Let me go, I say."

"I will not let you go until I want to," Orlando replied. "First, listen to me. My father charged you in his will to give me a good education; instead, you have trained me like a peasant, not allowing me the chance to acquire the accomplishments of a gentleman. The spirit of my father grows strong in me, and I will no longer endure your treatment; therefore, give me the education that a gentleman ought to have, or give me the small inheritance that my father left me in his will. With that small inheritance, I will leave here and seek my fortune elsewhere."

"And what will you do? Will you beg after you have spent your inheritance? Well, sir, go inside the house. I will not long be troubled with you; you shall have some part of what you want. Leave me now."

"I will bother you no more than is necessary to get what I need."

Oliver said to Adam, "Go with him, you old dog."

Adam said, "Is being called 'old dog' my reward for serving your family for decades? Truly, I have lost my teeth in your family's service. May God be with my old master! He would not have called me an old dog."

Orlando and Adam left the garden.

Alone, Oliver said, "So this is what it comes down to. It's a showdown between you and me. You have become a nuisance to me. You have grown wild, Orlando, but I will give you your medicine and curb your wildness. And that medicine will not be one thousand crowns."

He summoned a servant: "Come here, Dennis!"

Dennis arrived and asked, "How may I help you?"

"Isn't Charles, Duke Frederick's wrestler, here to speak with me?"

"Yes, he is here at the door and wants to speak with you."

"Call him in."

Dennis left to get Charles.

"This is a good way to solve my problem," Oliver said. "Tomorrow there will be wrestling."

Charles entered and said, "Good day to your worship."

"Good Monsieur Charles, what's the new news at the new court?"

"The news at the court," Charles said, "is the old news. Old Senior has been banished by his younger brother, Duke Frederick. Three or four lords who greatly respect Duke Senior have gone into exile — in their case, voluntarily — with him. Duke Frederick allowed them to go into exile so he could seize their lands and revenues and enrich himself."

"Can you tell me if Rosalind, Duke Senior's daughter, is banished with her father?"

"She has not been banished," Charles replied. "Duke Frederick's daughter, Celia, so loves Rosalind, with whom she has been friends since both were in the cradle, that Celia would have followed her into exile — or if prevented from following her, she would have died of grief. Rosalind is at the court, and her uncle, Duke Frederick, loves her no less than his own daughter, Celia — never have two ladies loved each other as Celia and Rosalind do."

"Where will the old Duke — Duke Senior — live?"

"People say that he is already in the Forest of Arden, and that he has many merry men with him, and there in the forest they live like the old Robin Hood of England. People say that many young gentlemen flock to him every day, and they spend the time without cares, as was the case in the Golden Age of classical mythology. They live without cares and with great ease."

"Will you wrestle tomorrow before Duke Frederick?"

"Yes, I will," Charles said. "In fact, this is why I am here. I have learned from secret sources that your younger brother Orlando intends to put on a disguise and wrestle against me. However, tomorrow, sir, I wrestle to protect and improve my reputation, and any wrestler who escapes from me without suffering a broken limb shall acquit himself well. Your brother is but young and tender, and out of respect for you, I am loath to defeat and injure him, as I must do, for my own reputation, if he wrestles against me. Therefore, because I respect you, I came here to tell you these things so that either you might convince him not to wrestle me or prepare yourself to endure disgrace when I defeat your youngest brother. A wrestling match between him and me is something that he — not I — wants. My wrestling your youngest brother is completely against my will."

"Charles, I thank you for your respect for and loyalty to me, which you will find I will most appropriately reward. I have previously learned of my brother's plan to wrestle you and I have tried unobtrusively to dissuade him from wrestling you, but he is determined to carry out his plan. I tell you, Charles, that my youngest brother is the most ruthless young fellow of all France. He is full of ambition, he envies every man's good qualities and abilities, and he is a secret and villainous contriver against me, his birth brother. Therefore, use your own discretion. As for myself, I would prefer that you break his neck than his finger. But be careful because if he thinks that you have defeated him by even by a little and if he fails to score a notable victory against you, he will plot against you and try to poison you. He will try to trap you with some treacherous plot, and he will never leave you alone until he has killed you by some indirect means or other so that he is not punished for your death. I am almost in tears as I tell you truly that no one as young and as villainous as Orlando is alive today. I am his brother, and I speak as a brother, but if I were to explain to you his real character in every detail, then I must blush and weep and you must look pale and wonder."

"I am heartily glad I came here and spoke to you," Charles said. "If Orlando comes to wrestle me tomorrow, I will give him his payment. If he ever again walks without crutches, I will retire from professional wrestling. May God bless you."

"Farewell, good Charles," Oliver said.

Charles left, and Oliver said to himself, "Now I will provoke this gamester — my youngest brother. I hope I shall see an end of him — his death. My soul, I do not know why, hates nothing more than him, yet he is endowed with the qualities of a gentleman. He has never been schooled and yet he is learned, and he is full of gentlemanliness. He is enchantingly — as if they were under a spell — beloved by all ranks of people, and indeed the world itself loves him. Especially my own subjects, who best know him, love him so much that they prefer him to me and they despise me. But this shall not last much longer. Charles the wrestler shall solve my problems. All that I need to do is to find Orlando and incite the boy to wrestle tomorrow, and I will go right now and do that."

— 1.2 —

On the lawn in front of the Duke's palace, Celia and Rosalind talked.

Celia said, "Please, dear cousin, be merry."

"Dear Celia, I already am showing more happiness than I feel, and yet you want me to appear to be even happier? Unless you can teach me to forget my banished father, you must not tell me to think about any extraordinary pleasure."

"Here I see that you do not love me as much as I love you," Celia said. "If my uncle, Duke Senior — who is your banished father — had banished your uncle, Duke Frederick — who is my father — as long as you stayed with me, I could have taught myself to regard your father as my father. You would do the same thing for me if you loved me as much as I love you."

"Well, I will forget the condition of my situation in life, so that I can rejoice in the condition of your situation in life."

"You know that my father has no child but me," Celia said, "and he is unlikely to have any more children. When my father dies, you shall be his heir because what he has taken away from your father by force, I will give to you. I swear it. If I break this oath, let me turn into a monster. Therefore, my sweet and dear Rose, be happy."

Rosalind replied, "From here on, I will, cousin, and I will think of games for us to play together. Let me see. What do you think about falling in love?"

"Go ahead and fall in love," Celia replied, "so we can laugh about it. But do not fall in love for real and in earnest. Fall in love no further than you can get out of love with an innocent blush and with your honor and reputation intact."

"What shall we do to amuse ourselves, then?"

"Let us sit and mock the good housewife — make that hussy — Fortune so that she turns away from the wheel that she spins and then gives either good or bad fortune according to the turn of the wheel. Once Fortune has abandoned her Wheel of Fortune, she will be forced to give away her gifts in equal measures."

"I wish that we could do that," Rosalind said, "because Fortune's gifts are mightily misplaced. Fortune is blind, and it shows when she gives gifts to women."

"That is true because those women whom Fortune makes beautiful she rarely makes virtuous, and those women she makes virtuous she usually makes ugly."

"No," Rosalind objected. "You are mixing up Fortune and Nature. Fortune determines whether we have good or bad fortune, and Nature makes us attractive or ugly."

Touchstone, a professional fool, aka court jester, walked close to Celia and Rosalind. His job was to make Duke Frederick and others laugh, and he got his name from a stone that was used to test the purity of gold and silver. To call Touchstone a fool was not really an insult — it was more of a job description like calling someone a tailor or cobbler. As a fool, Touchstone had the privilege to insult other people without being punished for it — although sometimes he could be threatened with punishment.

"Are you sure about that?" Celia asked. "Nature may make a woman beautiful, but Fortune may make her fall in a fire and mar her beauty. Nature may have given us enough wit and intelligence to mock Fortune, but did not Fortune send in this fool to stop our mocking her?"

"Indeed, Fortune is more powerful than Nature," Rosalind replied. "This is shown by Fortune sending in a fool to stop us from using our wits — our gifts from Nature — to make fun of Fortune."

"Perhaps this is not the work of Fortune," Celia said. "Perhaps Nature sees that our natural wits are too dull to discuss such goddesses as Fortune, and therefore Nature sent us this fool to be our whetstone and sharpen our wits instead of our knives. The dullness of a fool always sharpens the wits of other people."

Celia asked Touchstone, "Hello, wit. Where are you going?"

"Mistress, you must go to your father."

"What warrants making you the messenger?" Celia asked.

"I have no warrant for your arrest, but on my honor I was told to come to you and deliver a message."

"That's a fancy phrase: 'on my honor.' Where did you learn that phrase, fool?" Rosalind asked.

"I learned it from a certain knight who swore by his honor that the pancakes were good and swore by his honor that the mustard was bad. I disagree: The pancakes were bad and the mustard was good. Nevertheless, the knight did not commit perjury."

"Tell us your reasoning," Celia said. "Use the great heap of your knowledge to prove that the knight did not commit perjury."

"Yes, please prove that," Rosalind said. "Unmuzzle your wisdom."

"I will indeed," Touchstone said, "but first stroke your chins, and swear by your beards that I am a knave."

Celia replied, "By our beards, if we had them, we swear that you are a knave."

"If I were a knave, I would swear by my knavery that I am a knave. But I have no knavery. Anyone who swears by something that he or she does not have commits no perjury. This knight swore by his honor, but he had no honor. Either he never had any honor, or if he once had honor, he had sworn it away by breaking oaths before he ever saw those pancakes or that mustard."

"Please tell which knight you mean," Celia said.

"A knight whom old Frederick, your father, respects."

"In that case, my father's respect is enough to honor him, so enough! Talk no more about that knight — you will be whipped for slander one of these days."

"It is a pity that fools may not speak wisely about what wise men do foolishly. That is part of the job of a fool."

"You are saying the truth," Celia said. "A book burning was held recently, and many books of satire perished in the flames. Ever since then, the little wit that fools have has been silenced, and the little foolery that wise men have has become greatly more apparent. A fool who mocks the foolishness of wise men helps keep wise men wise."

She looked up and said, "Here comes Monsieur Le Beau."

Rosalind said, "He seems eager to tell us something. His mouth is full of news."

"He will force his news on us the way that parent pigeons force their nestlings to feed," Celia said.

"We will be force-fed and crammed with news."

"If we were birds or animals at the market, we would be more valuable because birds and animals are sold by weight," Celia said.

She greeted Monsieur Le Beau: "*Bon jour*, Monsieur. What's the news?"

"Fair princess, you have missed out on some good entertainment."

"Entertainment? What kind of entertainment?"

"I'm not quite sure how to answer that," Monsieur Le Beau said.

Rosalind said, "Answer it the way that your wit and fortune allow you to answer it."

"Or answer it as the Destinies decree," Touchstone said. "The Destinies are the Fates, and they rule our lives."

"Well said," Celia complimented Touchstone. "You are using a trowel to coat your words with learning."

"I am a jester," Touchstone said. "My rank is my reputation. I must keep up my rank."

"Unless you keep up your rankness, you won't be able to smell yourself," Rosalind joked.

Monsieur Le Beau said, "You amaze me, ladies. I wanted to tell you about some good wrestling that you are missing."

"Tell us what kind of wrestling," Rosalind said.

"I will tell you about the wrestling that has already happened, and if you want to, you can see the rest of the wrestling — the best part is yet to come," Monsieur Le Beau said. "Here, where you are now, is where the wrestling will take place."

"Tell us about the wrestling that is already over, that is dead and buried," Celia said.

Monsieur Le Beau began, "There comes an old man and his three sons —"

Celia interrupted him: "I could match this beginning with an old fairy tale. Many old fairy tales are about an old man and his three children."

"They are three proper young men, of excellent growth and presence."

"Presence?" Rosalind asked. "They must have had proclamations hanging from their necks — proclamations that begin, 'Be it known to all men by these presents — by this public proclamation ....'"

Monsieur Le Beau continued, "The eldest of the three sons wrestled with Charles, Duke Frederick's champion wrestler. Charles quickly threw him and broke three of his ribs. There is little hope that he will survive. Charles then did the same thing with the second son and the third son. They are still lying there. Their poor old father is crying with such grief that all the witnesses of the wrestling are crying with him."

Touchstone asked, "What is the entertainment that these ladies have been missing, Monsieur Le Beau?"

"Why, the wrestling that I have been talking about."

"Men may grow wiser everyday," Touchstone said. "This is the first time that I ever heard that the breaking of ribs was entertainment for ladies."

"It is also the first time that I have heard it," Celia said.

"Does anyone else want to see this wrestling and listen to the broken 'music' of breath performed with broken ribs?" Rosalind asked. "Is anyone else tempted to listen to the breaking of ribs? Celia, shall we see this wrestling?"

"You must see the wrestling, if you stay here," Monsieur Le Beau said. "This is the place where the wrestling will take place, and this is the time for the wrestling to start."

"That is true," Celia said. "I see that the wrestlers and the crowd are coming. Let us stay here and watch the match."

Duke Frederick, various Lords, Orlando, Charles, and many others walked over to Celia, Rosalind, Touchstone, and Monsieur Le Beau.

Duke Frederick said, "The youthful challenger — Orlando — is determined to wrestle Charles, although we have tried to dissuade him. His own recklessness is putting him in peril."

"Is he Orlando?" Rosalind said, gesturing to a man.

"Yes, he is, madam," Monsieur Le Beau said.

"It's a pity — he is too young," Celia said. "Yet he looks strong and like a wrestler. He looks as if he could defeat Charles."

"Hi, daughter and niece," Duke Frederick said. "Have you come here to see the wrestling?"

"Yes, my liege," Rosalind said, "as long as it's OK with you."

"You will take little delight in it, I can tell you," he said. "The odds are greatly against this young man. I would gladly convince Orlando not to wrestle Charles, but he won't listen to me. Speak to him, ladies; see if you can persuade him not to wrestle Charles."

"Bring Orlando over to us, good Monsieur Le Beau," Celia said.

Duke Frederick said to Monsieur Le Beau, "Do that. I will leave so that the princesses can talk to Orlando privately."

Monsieur Le Beau said to Orlando, "Challenger, the princesses want to talk to you."

"I will go to them with all the respect and duty that is due to them," Orlando replied.

Rosalind asked him, "Young man, have you challenged Charles the wrestler?"

"No, fair princess. Charles is the general challenger: He will wrestle anyone who wants to wrestle him. I came here like others to wrestle him and test the strength of my youth."

"Young gentleman, you are too bold for your age," Celia said to Orlando. "You have seen cruel proof of this man's strength in the number of ribs that he has broken. If you looked at yourself carefully and carefully considered what you are able to do, you would feel fear and choose another activity to engage in. Both of us ask you, for your own sake, to think about your own safety and not wrestle Charles."

"Do as Celia asks, young sir," Rosalind said. "Your reputation shall not be harmed by it. We will plead to Duke Frederick to stop the wrestling match before it starts. You will not be blamed for not wrestling Charles."

"Thank you, but no," Orlando said. "Do not regard me badly because I am refusing your request. I hate to deny anything to two such fair and excellent ladies as you. But let your fair eyes and gentle wishes go with me as I wrestle Charles. If Charles defeats me, then I will be the only one who is shamed, and I have never had good fortune anyway. If Charles kills me, then so be it. I am willing to die. I shall do my friends no wrong, for I have no friends to mourn me. I shall do the world no injury, for in the world I have nothing. In the world, I only fill up a space, and when I am dead, perhaps a better person will take my place."

Rosalind said, "The little strength that I have, I wish that I could give to you to help you in this match."

"And I wish that I could give you the little strength that I have," Celia said, "so it could be added to hers."

"Fare you well," Rosalind said. "I hope to God that you can defeat Charles although I know that the odds are against you."

"I hope that you get your heart's desire," Celia said.

Charles said loudly, "Let's get started. Where is the young gallant who is eager to be buried and lie with his mother Earth?"

"I am ready to wrestle you, sir," Orlando said, "but I am not ready to lie with my mother Earth. My goal is different."

Duke Frederick said, "This wrestling match will consist of only one round and one fall."

Charles boasted, "I am sure that you will not be able to persuade this man to undertake a second round although you could not dissuade him from undertaking a first round. I will defeat him so badly that he won't be able to wrestle a second round."

Orlando said to Charles, "You intend to mock me after the round, and that's OK if you can defeat me, but you should not mock me before the round. But let's get started."

"May Hercules, the strongest of the ancient Greek heroes, give you success," Rosalind said to Orlando.

"I wish I were invisible so I could grab the strong Charles by the leg and help Orlando," Celia said.

Charles and Orlando started to wrestle.

Rosalind said about Orlando, "He is an excellent young man!"

"If I had the Roman god Jupiter's power of hurling thunderbolts, I would shoot down Charles," Celia said.

Orlando threw Charles and won the wrestling match.

"No more!" Duke Frederick said. "The wrestling match is over."

"I am ready to wrestle some more," Orlando said. "I am not yet winded; in fact, I am not even properly warmed up."

"How are you, Charles?" Duke Frederick asked.

"He is unconscious and cannot speak, my Lord," Monsieur Le Beau said.

"Carry him away," Duke Frederick said.

He asked Orlando, "What is your name, young man?"

"Orlando, my Lord. I am the youngest son of Sir Rowland de Boys."

"I wish that you were the son of some other man. The world regarded your father as an honorable man, but I always found him to be my enemy. Your athletic victory today would have pleased me better if you were a member of some other family. But may you fare well; you are a gallant youth. Still, I wish that you had told me that another man is your father."

Most of the people present left, leaving behind Rosalind, Celia, and Orlando. Rosalind and Celia stood apart from Orlando.

Celia was disappointed in her father's reaction to learning who Orlando's father was. She felt that her father had been rude to Orlando.

She said to Rosalind, "If I were my father, I would have acted better than my father did."

Orlando said to himself, "I am very proud to be Sir Rowland's son, his youngest son, and I would not change that even to be Duke Frederick's adopted heir."

Rosalind said to Celia, "My father loved Sir Rowland as if Sir Rowland were his soul, and everyone else in the world shared my father's good opinion of Sir Rowland. Had I before known that this young man was his son, I would have added tears to my entreaties because of my fear that he would be injured or killed in this wrestling match."

Celia replied, "Gentle cousin, let us go and thank and encourage Orlando. My father's rough and malicious words to him wound me in my heart."

They went to Orlando, and Celia said, "Sir, you have well deserved this athletic victory. If you keep your promises in love as well as you keep your promises in wrestling — doing far more than anyone expected — your wife will be happy and fortunate."

Rosalind removed a necklace from her neck and gave it to Orlando, saying, "Wear this for me: a woman who is out of favor with fortune. I wish that I could give you more, but I lack more to give."

Rosalind expected Orlando to thank her, but he only stared at her.

She said to Celia, "Shall we go, cousin?"

Celia replied, "Yes."

To Orlando, Celia said, "Fare you well, fair gentleman."

Orlando did not reply to the two young women. Already, he was in love with Rosalind, and he found himself unable to speak. He was brave enough to wrestle Charles, Duke Frederick's champion wrestler, but he was not brave enough to speak to Rosalind.

But Orlando did reprimand himself, to himself, "Can't I even say, 'I thank you?' My bravery has disappeared, and the man I am right now is only a mannequin, a mere lifeless block."

Already, Rosalind was in love with Orlando. Hearing him mutter to himself, she said to Celia, "He is calling for us to come back to him."

Eager to talk to Orlando, she said to herself, "My good fortune left me earlier in life. Now I am losing my pride and chasing this young man. I will ask him what he wants."

Rosalind asked Orlando, "Did you call, sir? Sir, you have wrestled well and overthrown more than your enemies."

She thought, *That's a pretty good hint to him that he has overthrown me and that I am in love with him.*

Poor Orlando could not speak; he could only stare.

Celia said to Rosalind, "Are you ready to go now?"

Rosalind replied to her, "Yes, I am ready."

To Orlando, she said, "Fare you well."

As Rosalind and Celia left, Rosalind thought, *Orlando needs to be educated in romance. For one more thing, he has to learn how to be comfortable when talking to a young woman he likes. Unless he can do that, he will not go far in love. Unless he is comfortable when talking to a young woman he likes, he is unlikely ever to be the father of her children.*

If Orlando could have heard Rosalind's thoughts, he would have agreed with her. He said to himself, "What passion hangs these weights upon my tongue? I could not speak to Rosalind, although she wanted me to speak to her. Poor Orlando, you have been overthrown! Charles could not defeat you, but this much weaker woman has conquered you."

Monsieur Le Beau walked up to Orlando and said, "Good sir, I do in friendship advise you to leave this place. Although you have earned and deserve high praise, true applause, and respect, yet Duke Frederick is now of such a temperament that he misinterprets all that you have done. It is better for you to imagine the kind of person Duke Frederick is than for me to tell you."

"I thank you, sir," Orlando replied, adding, "Please, tell me this: Which of the two young women who were here at the wrestling match is the daughter of Duke Frederick?"

"Fortunately, neither of the two young women has Duke Frederick's bad manners," Monsieur Le Beau replied, "but the shorter of the two is his daughter, Celia. The other, taller young woman is the daughter of the banished Duke Senior. Her name is Rosalind, and her usurping uncle is keeping her here to keep his daughter company. The two young women love each other more than sisters do. However, I can tell you that Duke Frederick has recently taken a dislike to Rosalind, his well-born niece, for no other reason than that the citizens praise her for her virtues and pity her for her good father's sake. I swear by my own life that quickly Duke Frederick's hatred for Rosalind will erupt. Sir, farewell. Later, in a better world, I would like to know you better."

"I am much obliged to you," Orlando said. "Goodbye."

Monsieur Le Beau left.

Orlando said to himself, "Now I must go from the frying pan into the fire. I must go from the tyrant Duke Frederick to my tyrant eldest brother, Oliver. And, oh, I am in love with the Heavenly Rosalind."

— 1.3 —

In a room of Duke Frederick's palace, Rosalind and Celia were talking.

Celia said to Rosalind, "Why, cousin! You are so quiet! May Cupid, the god of love, have mercy on you! Can't you speak a word?"

"You have heard of people who are so poor that they aren't even able to throw scraps of food to a dog. I am not able to throw even a word to a dog."

"Your words are too precious to be cast away upon curs," Celia said. "Throw some of your words at me. Some people throw rocks at dogs to maim them and make them lame, so come, throw your words at me and lame me."

"If I did that, both of us would then be hurt. You would be lamed with words, and I would be crazy."

"Are you depressed because of your father?"

"Yes, but I am also depressed because of the man who should be the father of my child, when I have one. I am crazy in love with someone who can't even speak to me. Right now, the world is wearisome and full of briers."

"They are only burs, cousin, that have been thrown at you because of your foolish behavior when you chased after a man as if you were on a holiday. Act conventionally, and you will not suffer in this way. Unless we walk in the well-trodden paths, our petticoats will catch burs."

"I could shake those burs off the bottoms of my petticoats; these burs are in my heart."

"Hem them away."

"I could 'him' them away, if I could have Orlando."

"Come, come, wrestle with your affections."

"My affections are for a better wrestler than myself!"

"If you get your wish, eventually you will wrestle him, with you lying flat on your back with your legs apart," Celia said. "But let us put aside these jokes and instead talk earnestly. Is it really possible, that you — so suddenly — have fallen in love with old Sir Rowland's youngest son?"

"Duke Senior, my father, loved his father dearly."

"Does it therefore follow that you should love his son dearly? By this kind of argument, I should hate Orlando because my father hated his father dearly, but I do not hate Orlando."

"No, do not hate Orlando — for my sake."

"Why shouldn't I hate Orlando? By this kind of argument, I ought to hate him — by this kind of argument, he deserves my hatred."

"Let me love him because he deserves my love. You can love him because I love him."

Rosalind added, "Look, here comes your father, Duke Frederick."

"His eyes are full of anger," Celia said.

Duke Frederick and some Lords entered the room.

Duke Frederick said to Rosalind, "Madam, as quickly as you safely can, get out of my court."

"Do you mean me, uncle?"

"Yes, I mean you, niece. If, after ten days, you are found within twenty miles of my court, you will die."

"Please, uncle, tell me the nature of my offence. Tell me what I have done wrong. If I know my own thoughts and desires — if I am not dreaming or insane, and I don't think that I am — then I, dear uncle, have never come close to thinking or desiring anything that would offend you."

"So say all traitors," Duke Frederick replied. "If they could be cleared by their own words, all of them would be as innocent as virtue itself. Let me tell you plainly that I do not trust you."

"Even your mistrust cannot make me a traitor: Tell me the grounds on which you believe that I am a traitor."

"You are your father's daughter. That is enough reason to think that you are a traitor."

"I was my father's daughter when you took his Dukedom," Rosalind said. "I was my father's daughter when you banished him. Treason is not inherited, my Lord. But even if treason were contagious and we did catch it from our friends, how does that apply to me? My father was no traitor. My good Lord, do not think that my poverty has made me a traitor. Although I am poor, I am not a traitor."

"Dear sovereign father, listen to me," Celia said.

"Celia, I have allowed Rosalind to stay here for your sake. If not for you, I would have made her go with her father when he went into exile."

"I did not then beg you to have Rosalind stay here. That was your own decision, made because you yourself wanted her to stay and because you felt remorse for your own actions. I was too young at that time to value Rosalind, but now I know her. If she is a traitor, then so am I. We always have slept together, gotten up together, been educated together, eaten together, and wherever we went, we went together and inseparable, like the two swans that pull the chariot in which Juno, the Roman goddess of marriage, rides."

"Rosalind is too cunning for you," Duke Frederick replied. "Her deceptive charm, her silence, and her patience appeal to the people, and they pity her. You are a fool: She robs you of your reputation — you will appear brighter and seem more virtuous after she is gone. So do not open your lips. Firm and irrevocable are the judgment and the punishment that I have given to her. She is banished from my Dukedom."

"Then give me the same judgment and punishment," Celia said. "I cannot live without Rosalind's companionship."

"You are a fool," Duke Frederick said to Celia.

He said to Rosalind, "You, niece, prepare yourself for your journey into exile. If you are still here after ten days, I swear that you will die."

He and the other Lords left the room.

"Oh, my poor Rosalind," Celia said, "where will you go? Are you willing to exchange fathers? I will give you my father in return for your father. Please, do not be more grieved than I am."

"I have more cause for grief."

"No, you don't," Celia said. "Be cheerful. Don't you know that my father, Duke Frederick, has banished me?"

"No, he has not."

"Hasn't he? You, Rosalind, lack the love that ought to teach you that you and I are one. Shall we be sundered? Shall we be parted, sweet girl? No. Let my father seek another heir. Therefore plan with me how we may flee into exile. Let us plan where to go and what to take with us. Do not seek to go alone, to bear your griefs by yourself and leave me here. I swear by the Heavens, which have grown pale because of our sorrows, that no matter what you say, I will go with you into exile."

"Where shall we go?" Rosalind asked.

"To seek my uncle — your father — in the Forest of Arden."

"We will be in danger. We are two young virgins traveling so far alone! Our feminine beauty will make us even more of a target for criminals than money alone would."

"I will wear poor and mean clothing and with a kind of brown paint will darken my face to make myself look like a peasant instead of a court lady. You can do the same thing. If we look like poor peasants, we shall be able to travel and never be bothered by assailants."

"Wouldn't it better," Rosalind replied, "if, because I am tall for a woman, I were to dress and act like a man? I could carry a gallant short sword upon my thigh, a boar-spear in my hand, and a swashing and martial outside appearance, while I hide in my heart whatever womanish fears I feel. I will do what other cowards do — I will act as if I am brave when I do not feel brave at all. And you and I could be brother and sister."

"What shall I call you when you are dressed like a man?"

"I'll have no worse a name than the god Jupiter's own page," Rosalind said. "He saw a boy named Ganymede and kidnapped him to be his cup-bearer. Therefore, call me Ganymede. But what name will you take?"

"I will take a name that is suitable to my new situation in life. I will no longer be called Celia. Instead, call me Aliena — the Estranged One. My father and I are now estranged."

"Cousin, here's a good idea. Let's take Touchstone the fool with us when we leave your father's court. Wouldn't he be a comfort as we travel?"

"He will be happy to go with me and travel the wide world with me," Celia said to Rosalind. "Leave it to me to talk to him. Let us go now and get our jewels and our wealth together. We will plan the best time and the safest way to leave so that we will escape the pursuit that will be made after my father discovers that I have gone into exile with you. Now we can go contently — we are going into liberty and not into banishment."

CHAPTER 2

— 2.1 —

Duke Senior, the Lord Amiens, and a few other Lords were talking together in the Forest of Arden. All of them were dressed like foresters.

Duke Senior said, "Now, my companions and brothers in exile, have we not grown used to our new way of life and don't we now agree that this way of life is better than a life of artificial splendor? Are not these woods freer from danger than the envious and malicious court? Here we feel only the penalty of Adam, who was sent away from the Garden of Eden into exile. We feel the different seasons, such as the icy fang and churlish chiding of the winter's wind, which, when it bites and blows upon my body, even as I shrink with cold, I smile and say, 'This is no flattery: These are counselors who powerfully tell me what I really am.' Sweet are the uses of adversity — adversity makes men wise. Adversity is like an ugly toad that according to folklore is poisonous and yet has a jewel — the toadstone — in its head that protects itself and others from poison. Our life is free from interruption from other people, and here we can listen to the trees, read the running brooks, and learn about natural theology from stones. Everything here in Nature is good."

Amiens, a Lord who had followed Duke Senior into exile and who was a good singer, said, "I would not change anything. Happy is your grace, who can translate the harshness of fortune into so quiet and so sweet a state of mind. You are able to look at bad fortune and see what good may come from it."

"Come, shall we go and kill us a deer and eat venison?" Duke Senior asked. "And yet it irks me that the poor dappled fools, being native citizens of this scarcely populated territory, should in their own land have their round haunches gored with arrowheads."

A Lord said, "Indeed, Duke Senior, the melancholy Jaques grieves at that, also, and accordingly, he swears that you do more usurp the deer's territory than your younger brother, Duke Frederick, usurped your territory when he banished you. Today my Lord of Amiens and I did creep up behind Jaques as he lay under an oak whose ancient root pokes out near the brook that flows noisily through this wood. To that place came a poor stag that had been separated from its herd. A hunter had wounded it, and indeed, my Lord, the wretched animal heaved forth such groans that their discharge did stretch his leathern coat until it seemed that he would burst his hide, and the stag's big round tears trickled down his innocent nose as they chased each other, arousing pity. The melancholy Jaques looked at the hairy stag as it stood on the edge of the brook and added its tears to the brook's water."

"What did Jaques say?" Duke Senior asked. "Knowing him, he would have drawn moral lessons from this stag's suffering."

The Lord replied, "You are correct. Jaques made a thousand similes. Seeing the stag dropping his tears into the stream, Jaques said, 'Poor deer, you are making a last will and testament the way that materialistic humans do. You give more to what already has too much. The stream of water hardly needs your tears.' Seeing the stag alone, abandoned by its herd, Jaques said, 'Misery stops a stream of visitors. A poor or ill person has few visitors.' Soon, a carefree herd of deer that had eaten its fill of grass in a meadow ran by the wounded stag and did not stop to greet him. Seeing this, Jaques said, 'Run on, you fat and greasy citizens. This is the current fashion. Why should you bother to look upon this poor and broken wretch here?' Thus he harshly criticized and pierced the heart of the country, city, court, and even our way of life here. He swore that we are mere usurpers and tyrants and whatever is worse than usurpers and tyrants, because we frighten the animals and kill them in their Heavenly assigned and native dwelling places."

"Did you leave him to his contemplations?" Duke Senior asked.

A second Lord said, "We did, my Lord. He was weeping and commenting on the sobbing deer."

"Show me where he is," Duke Senior said. "I love to debate him when he is in one of these moralizing moods because then he has a lot to say."

The first Lord said, "I will take you to him right away."

— 2.2 —

In a room in his palace, Duke Frederick questioned some Lords.

"Is it possible that no one saw Celia and Rosalind leave the palace? It cannot be. Some villains in my court knew about this and assisted them."

A Lord said, "I cannot find anyone who saw your daughter leave. The ladies, her attendants of her chamber, saw her go to bed in the evening, and early in the morning, they found her bed empty."

Another Lord said, "Duke Frederick, the vulgar and despicable clown at whom so often you have been accustomed to laugh is also missing. Hisperia, the princess Celia's gentlewoman, confesses that she secretly overheard Celia and Rosalind much compliment the good qualities and accomplishments of Orlando, the wrestler who recently defeated the sinewy Charles. Hisperia believes that wherever Celia and Rosalind are gone, Orlando is surely with them."

Duke Frederick said, "Send someone to Orlando's brother Oliver. The messenger must bring Orlando to me, or if Orlando is gone, the messenger must bring Oliver to me. I will make Oliver find Orlando. Do this at once. Meanwhile, we will continue to inquire after and search for these foolish runaways and bring them back."

— 2.3 —

In front of Oliver's house, Orlando and the family's aged servant, Adam, met.

Orlando asked, "Who's there?"

Recognizing Orlando's voice, Adam said, "My young master! My gentle master! My sweet master! You memory of old Sir Rowland! Why, what are you doing here? Why are you so virtuous? Why do people love you so much? And why are you gentle, strong, and valiant? Why were you so foolish that you defeated the strong wrestler of the moody Duke Frederick? Your praise has come home before you have come home. Don't you know, master, that for some men virtues and accomplishments are dangerous to have because they make other people jealous and murderous? Your virtues and accomplishments are like that. Gentle master, your virtues and accomplishments are sanctified and holy traitors to you. What kind of a world is this, when what is good and beautiful in a man poisons him and leads to his death!"

"What's the matter? What's going on?" Orlando asked.

"Unhappy youth!" Adam replied. "Don't come inside here. Under this roof lives someone who is the enemy of all your good qualities. Your brother — no, he does not act like a brother. Yet he is the son — but no, I won't call him the son of the man I was about to call his father. But under this roof lives someone who has heard the praise you received for defeating Charles, and this night he means to burn down the place where you are accustomed to sleep and so kill you. If he fails to kill you that way, he has other ways to stop your heart. I overheard him and his plans. This house is no home; this house is a slaughterhouse. Abhor it, fear it, and do not enter it."

"Then where, Adam, do you think I should go?"

"It does not matter where you go, as long as you don't come here."

"Do you want me to become a beggar and beg for my food? Or do you want me to make a living as a thief wielding a base and violent sword on the highway? To live, I must do these things — I don't know any other way to make my living. Yet I will not become either a beggar or a robber, no matter what. I prefer to subject myself to the malice of a bloodthirsty brother who does not treat me as a brother."

"Don't do that," Adam said. "I have five hundred crowns, money that I thriftily saved from my wages while I worked for your father. I saved up this money to live on in my old age when my old limbs would lie lame and forgotten in some corner. Take this money. God, Who feeds the ravens and providently cares for the sparrow, will be my comfort in my old age! Here is the gold — all this I give to you. Let me be your servant and accompany you in your journey. Though I look old, I am still strong and healthy. In my youth I never drank alcohol and I never lived recklessly and shamefully in such a way that would make me weak and debilitated. Therefore, my old age is like a vigorous winter — it is frosty, but kindly. Therefore, let me go with you. I will do the service of a younger man in whatever needs to be done."

Adam had studied Psalm 147:9 and Luke 12:6 and Luke 12:24:

Psalm 147:9: "He giveth to the beast his food, and to the young ravens which cry."

Luke 12:6: "Are not five sparrows sold for two farthings, and not one of them is forgotten before God?"

Luke 12:24: "Consider the ravens: for they neither sow nor reap; which neither have storehouse nor barn; and God feedeth them: how much more are ye better than the fowls?"

Orlando replied, "Good old man, in you I see the faithful service of the ancient world. At that time, people worked out of a sense of duty and not only for money. You don't follow the custom of these days when no one will work except for a promotion, and once they have the promotion, they stop working so hard. You are not like such people. But by serving me, you are pruning a rotten tree that cannot yield even a blossom in return for all your pains and husbandry. But come with me. We will travel together, and before we have spent your life savings, we will find a steady, sober, and humble way of life."

"Master, lead, and I will follow you to the last gasp, with truth and loyalty. From when I was seventeen years old until now when I am almost fourscore years old, I have lived here, but now I will live here no more. When they are seventeen years old, many people seek their fortunes, but at fourscore years old it is far too late for me to do so. Still, my fate cannot be better than to die well and not in my master's debt."

Adam was a faithful steward. He served the right master and not the wrong master.

— 2.4 —

Rosalind, Celia, and Touchstone were walking together. Rosalind, dressed like a young man, was going by the name Ganymede. Celia, dressed like a young peasant woman, was going by the name Aliena.

Rosalind said, "By Jupiter, how weary I am in spirit!"

"Ganymede, I would not care about my spirit, if my legs were not so weary," Touchstone said.

Rosalind said, "I could disgrace my man's clothing and cry like a woman, but I must comfort the weaker vessel because a man's jacket and trousers ought to be more courageous than a petticoat; therefore, be courageous, good Aliena!"

"Please bear with me," Celia said. "I cannot go any further."

They stopped walking.

Touchstone said, "For my part, Aliena, I had rather bear with you than bear you — I do not want to carry you. Still, I should bear no cross if I did bear you because I think you have no Elizabethan coins bearing a cross as a decoration in your purse."

Rosalind looked around and said, "Well, this is the Forest of Arden."

"Now I am in the Forest of Arden," Touchstone said. "Well, I am a bigger fool now than I was at home. When I was at home, I was in a better place; still, travellers have to be content with what they find."

"That's good advice, Touchstone," Rosalind said. "Please take it."

Corin, an old shepherd, and Silvius, a young shepherd who was in love with a young shepherdess named Phoebe, walked into the travelers' sight and hearing.

Rosalind said, "Look, two men are coming here. They are a young man and an old man talking earnestly."

Corin said to Silvius, "That is the way to make her scorn you always."

"Corin, I wish that you knew how much I love her!"

"I can partly guess because I have been in love before."

"No, Corin, you are old, and so you can not guess how much I love her — even if in your youth you were as true a lover as ever sighed upon a pillow at midnight as you thought about your love. If your love was ever like my love —

but I am sure that no man ever loved any woman as much as I love Phoebe — then how many really ridiculous actions did you do because of your love?"

"They run into a thousand really ridiculous actions that I have forgotten."

"Then you never did love as heartily as I love! Unless you remember even the slightest folly that love has made you commit, you have not loved. If you have never sat as I do now, wearying your hearer by constantly praising your loved one, you have not loved. If you have not run away from your friends abruptly, as my love now makes me do, you have not loved."

Silvius ran away, crying the name of the woman he loved: "Phoebe! Phoebe! Phoebe!"

Rosalind watched him run away, and then she said, "Poor shepherd! After learning about your lovesickness, I now am feeling my own. You have probed your wound, and now I feel the pain of my wound."

"And I am remembering my own lovesickness," Touchstone said, satirizing being in love. "I remember that when I was in love I broke my sword on a stone and told him 'Take that!' for coming at night because of Jane Smile. Yes, I had to beat my genitalia each night because of Jane Smile. I remember kissing her wooden beater for washing clothes and kissing the cow's udders that her pretty chapped hands had milked. I remember wooing a pea plant as a substitute for Jane Smile. I took two peascods from the plant and then I gave them back to the plant, weeping tears and saying, 'Wear these for my sake.' If Jane Smile were to accept a gift from me, that would mean that she was giving me permission to woo her. And if cods are testicles and peas are a piece, aka a penis, her wearing them would make me happy. And yes, every man needs a codpiece."

Touchstone paused, and then added, "We who are true lovers do strange things, but as all is mortal in nature, so is all nature in love mortal in folly. As all who love must die, so all who love must act foolishly. Love makes us do foolish things, but love also means that we are a part of the natural order."

Rosalind said, "You are speaking wiser than you are aware of."

"Aware or beware?" Touchstone asked. "I shall never beware of my own wit until I hurt my shins by banging up against it."

"The lovesickness of this young shepherd is much like my own," Rosalind said.

"And his lovesickness is like mine, but my lovesickness is growing stale," Touchstone said.

Celia said, "Please, will one of you ask that man over there if he will sell us any food? I am faint from hunger and feel as if I am almost dying."

Touchstone had little respect for rural countrymen; he regarded them all as hicks. He called to Corin, using an insulting term: "Hey, you clown!"

"By quiet, fool," Rosalind said to Touchstone. "He is not your kinsman. He is not a professional fool."

Corin replied, "Who is calling?"

Touchstone replied, "Your betters, sir."

To himself, Corin said, "If they were not my betters, they would be very wretched indeed."

To Touchstone, Rosalind said, "Be quiet."

To Corin, Rosalind said, "Good evening to you, friend."

"And to you, gentle sir," Corin replied courteously, "and to you all."

"Please, shepherd," Rosalind said, "if either courtesy or money can in this deserted place buy hospitality, take us to a place where we may rest ourselves and eat. Here is a young maiden much exhausted by travel; she is fainting from hunger."

"Fair sir, I pity her and I wish, for her sake more than for my own, I was better able to relieve her than I am, but I am a shepherd who works for another man and I do not get the wool from the sheep I shear. The wool and profit belong to my master, who has a churlish disposition and cares little about finding his way to Heaven by doing deeds of hospitality. Besides, his cottage, his flocks, and his pastureland are now for sale, and at our cottage now, because my master is away, there is nothing for refined people to eat. But come and see for yourself what food is there. As for myself, I will make you very welcome there."

"Who is the person who is thinking of buying his flock and pasture?" Rosalind asked.

"That young lover whom you saw here but a moment ago, but he is only thinking about it. I don't expect him to make a real offer to buy them."

"Please, if you can do so ethically and without taking advantage of the young shepherd," Rosalind said, "buy for us the cottage, the flock, and the pastureland, and we will pay for them."

Celia added, "And we will increase your wages. I like this place, and I willingly could spend my time here."

Corin was willing to buy the place for them. He said, "Assuredly this place is to be sold. Come with me. If you like what you see of the land, the profit that can be made, and this kind of life, I will be your very faithful shepherd and buy it with your gold right away."

They followed Corin.

— 2.5 —

In another part of the Forest of Arden, Jaques and some other lords listened to Amiens sing this song:

"*Under the greenwood tree*
"*Whoever loves to lie with me,*
"*And turn his merry note*
"*Unto the sweet bird's throat,*
"*Come here, come here, come here.*
"*Here shall he see*
"*No enemy*
"*But winter and rough weather.*"

The song celebrated the good parts of living in the Forest of Arden — love and singing and birdsong — while acknowledging the bad parts — winter and rough weather. In the Forest of Arden, the enemies are winter and rough weather. In the court, in contrast, the enemies can be much worse.

Jaques requested, "Sing more, more, please, more."

"My singing more will make you melancholy, Monsieur Jaques. You will become sad."

"So be it," Jaques said. "I enjoy melancholy. Sing more, please, more. I can suck melancholy out of a song, just like a weasel sucks eggs. More, please, more."

"My voice is ragged. I know I cannot please you."

"I do not want you to please me. I want you to sing. Come, more — sing me another stanzo. Do you call them stanzos?"

"Call them by whatever name you want, Jaques," Amiens replied.

"No, I don't care about their names — they are not written on an IOU, and so they owe me nothing. A list of names of sections of music is not very useful; a list of people who owe me money would be very useful indeed. Will you sing?"

"Yes, but I will sing more at your request than to please myself."

"Well, then, if ever I thank any man, I will thank you. But what people call thanks nowadays is like the encounter of two dog-faced baboons, who bow to each other by rote and without meaning it. Whenever a man thanks me heartily, I feel as if I have given him a penny and he is thanking me with the overenthusiastic thanks a beggar uses to thank someone who gives him money. But come, Amiens, sing."

To the other Lords, Jaques said, "All of you who will not be singing, please be quiet."

"Well, I'll finish singing the song," Amiens said. "Sirs, finish the preparation of the meal for Duke Senior and us. Place a blanket on the ground. Duke Senior will drink under this tree."

Amiens said to Jaques, "Duke Senior has spent all day looking for you."

"And I have spent all day avoiding him," Jaques replied. "He is too eager to debate me, in my opinion. I think of as many issues and topics as he does, but I just give Heaven thanks for my ideas — I do not feel that I need to show them off or boast about them. But, please, sing and warble."

Amiens sang, "*Whoever shuns ambition —*"

Everyone joined in and sang with Amiens:

"*And loves to live in the Sunshine,*
"*Seeking the food he eats*
"*And pleased with what he gets,*
"*Come here, come here, come here.*
"*Here shall he see*
"*No enemy*
"*But winter and rough weather.*"

Jaques said, "Now let me sing some additional words to this song. I wrote these words yesterday although I do not have a lot of creativity."

"And I'll sing it," Amiens said.

Jaques said, "It goes like this:

"*If it comes to pass*
"*That any man acts like an ass,*
"*Leaving his wealth and ease,*
"*A stubborn will to please,*
"*Ducdame, ducdame, ducdame:*
"*Here shall he see*
"*Fools as gross as he,*
"*If he will come to me.*"

The other Lords had moved closer to Jaques. They were in a circle around him.

"What does 'ducdame' mean?" Amiens asked.

Jaques replied, "It is a Greek — as in 'It's Greek to me' — magic spell used to gather fools in a circular formation."

He paused, and then said, "Well, I'll take a nap. If I can't go to sleep, I will find something else to do — I'll rail against all the first-born of Egypt. Exodus 11:5 states, 'And all the firstborn in the land of Egypt shall die, from the firstborn of Pharaoh that sitteth upon his throne, even unto the firstborn of the maidservant that is behind the mill; and all the firstborn of beasts.' Exodus 12:29-30 states, 'And it came to pass, that at midnight the LORD smote all the firstborn in the land of Egypt, from the firstborn of Pharaoh that sat on his throne unto the firstborn of the captive that was in the dungeon; and all the firstborn of cattle. During the night Pharaoh got up, he along with all his officials and all the Egyptians, and there was a loud wailing throughout Egypt because there wasn't a house without someone dead.' As for myself, I will rail against the first-born Duke Senior, who has had bad fortune and become a gypsy and led his followers — now also gypsies — into the wilderness. I will rail against him if I can't sleep because if I cannot, it will be because his followers have woken me up so Duke Senior can talk to me."

Amiens said, "I will find Duke Senior. The meal is prepared."

— 2.6 —

Nor far from the place where the meal had been prepared for Duke Senior and his followers, Orlando and Adam were walking, exhausted and hungry.

Adam said to Orlando, "Dear master, I can go no further. I am dying of hunger. I will lie down here, and my grave will be here. Farewell, kind master."

Orlando replied, "You must have more courage now. Live a little longer; be comforted a little; cheer yourself up a little. If this wild and uncultivated forest has anything savage in it, I will either be food for it or kill it and bring it here as food for you. Your imagination is making you think that you are closer to dying than you really are. For my sake, be comforted. Hold off death awhile and keep death at arm's length. I will return here and be with you soon, and if I don't bring you something to eat, I will give you permission to die, but if you die before I return, you will have mocked my efforts."

Adam nodded and Orlando said, "Well done! You look more cheerful, and I will return to you quickly. Yet you are lying in the cold air. I will carry you to some shelter. You will not die for lack of a dinner, if anything lives in this lonely forest. Be of good cheer, good Adam!"

— 2.7 —

Amiens had arrived with Duke Senior at the place where the meal was waiting. Jaques was out of sight.

"I have been searching for Jaques," Duke Senior said. "I think that he must be transformed into a beast because I can find the man nowhere."

A Lord said, "My Lord, he was here a moment ago. He was happy and playful, and he was listening to a song."

"Are you really talking about Jaques, the melancholy man?" Duke Senior asked. "If he, who is full of melancholy and of discords, becomes musical, very soon the music made by the spheres as they move in the sky will become discordant. Go and find him. I want to talk to him."

Jaques walked up to the group, and the Lord said, "He has saved me the trouble of finding him. Here he comes."

"How are you, monsieur?" Duke Senior said. "What kind of a life is this when your poor friends must seek you and beg for your company? Why, you look happy!"

Jaques was happy; he had met Touchstone, who had been wearing the motley costume that identified him as a professional fool. The cottage that Rosalind and Celia had bought was near Duke Senior's camp.

He said, "A fool, a fool! I met a fool in the forest, a motley fool — a fool wearing motley! It is a miserable world in which your friends must seek you and beg for your company, but as I do live by eating food, I met a fool who lay down and warmed himself in the Sunshine, and he criticized Lady Fortune with carefully chosen words and with rhetorical eloquence, and yet he was a motley fool.

"I said to him, 'Good day, fool,' but he replied to me, 'No, sir, fortune favors fools, so do not call me a fool until Heaven has sent me good fortune.'

"And then the fool took a watch from his pouch, and looking on it with lackluster eye, said very wisely, 'It is ten o'clock. Thus we may see how the world goes. It is but an hour ago since it was nine, and after one hour more it will be eleven. And so, from hour to hour, we grow riper and riper — more mature and more mature — and then, from hour to hour, we rot and rot, and thereby hangs a moral tale.'"

Jaques thought, *If instead of using the word "hour," the fool had used the word "whore," he would have said, "And so, from whore to whore, we rut and rut, and then, from whore to whore, we rot and rot with venereal disease, and thereby hangs an anatomical tail." The anatomical tail, of course, would be a penis.*

Jaques continued, "When I heard the motley fool thus moralize on the times, my lungs began to crow like the rooster named Chanticleer in Chaucer's 'Nun's Priest's Tale.' I was impressed that fools should be so deeply contemplative, and I laughed without intermission for an hour by his watch. What a noble fool! What a worthy fool! Motley is the only clothing to wear."

"Which fool are you talking about?" Duke Senior asked.

"He is a worthy fool!" Jaques said. "He has been a courtier at court, and he says that if ladies are young and beautiful, they always know it, and his brain, which is as dry as the left-over biscuit that remains after a long sea voyage, is crammed with strange topics and observations, which he utters in mangled forms and with dry wit. I wish I were a fool! My ambition is to wear a motley coat."

"You shall have one," Duke Senior said.

"It is my only suit — my only request to you and the only outfit I will need to wear," Jaques said, "provided that you get rid of any thoughts that I am wise. Such thoughts are rank and need to be weeded. I must have the freedom — a license as free as the wind — to blow my criticisms on whomever I please. That is the job of fools. Those people who are most galled with my satiric criticisms must laugh the hardest. Why, sir, must they laugh so hard? The 'why' is as plain as the way to the parish church: He whom a fool does very wisely hit with criticism will act wisely, although he is hurt by the criticism, to appear not to be hurt by the criticism. They will act foolishly if they allow their hurt to show. Wise men will appear not to smart from the satiric criticism, although they do in fact smart. Unless a man appears to appreciate the jokes, other people will think that the jokes were aimed at him, and the wise man's folly will be laid bare by the random satirical hits of the motley fool. So give me a motley costume and permission to speak my mind, and I will use satire to thoroughly cleanse the foulness from throughout the infected world if people will patiently receive my medicine."

"Don't be silly!" Duke Senior said. "I can tell you what you would do."

Jaques replied, "For less than two cents, tell me your thoughts."

"You would commit a most mischievous foul sin when you would chide the sins of other people," Duke Senior said. "An old proverb says, 'He finds fault with others and does worse himself.' You yourself have been a libertine. You have been as sensual as the brutish sting of animal lust itself. All the swollen sores and evils that have come to a head like boils, that you with your freedom and immorality have caught, you would vomit into the whole world."

Jaques ignored Duke Senior's criticism of his past and returned to his defense of satire: "How can anyone who denounces pride in general be said to have denounced any person in particular? Pride is as huge as the sea, and trying to indulge one's pride uses up all the resources available. What particular woman in the city do I name when I say that the women of the city bear the cost of princes on their unworthy shoulders by spending too much on expensive clothing as they try to appear to be of a higher class than they are? Who can come in and say that I mean her, when both she and her neighbor are doing exactly the same thing? Or what about a person who thinks that I am criticizing him in particular? He has a lowly job but dresses in expensive clothing — suppose he tells me that I don't pay for his expensive clothing and therefore it is of no concern to me. How can he say that without admitting that my criticism of him is true? What about that? How have my words hurt him? If my criticism is just, then he deserves the criticism. If he does not deserve the criticism and is free of sin, then my criticism will fly past him like a wild goose and will not harm him."

Jaques heard a noise, looked around, and said, "But look, someone is coming."

With his sword drawn, Orlando walked toward the group.

Orlando ordered, "Stop, and eat no more."

"Why, I have eaten nothing yet," Jaques said.

"Nor shall you, until those who most need the food have eaten," Orlando said.

"What cocky young man is this?" Jaques asked.

Duke Senior asked Orlando, "What makes you so rude and so bold, man? Are you in distress, or do you simply hate good manners?"

"I am in distress," Orlando replied. "The thorny point of bare distress has taken away from me the use of smooth good manners and civility. However, I was brought up in civilized society and I have had some good breeding. But again, I say, don't eat anything. Anyone who touches any of this fruit will die — they must wait to eat until I and my needs have been satisfied."

Jaques said, "If you will not be answered with reasons, I must die. But if reasons are not sufficient, perhaps raisins will be. Raisins make up part of our meal."

"What do you want?" Duke Senior said to Orlando. "Your gentleness shall force us more to help you than your force shall move us to gentleness. If you are polite, that will persuade us more quickly to give you what you need than your threatening us will persuade us to give you what you need."

"I am close to dying of hunger; therefore, let me have food," Orlando said.

"Sit down and eat, and welcome to our meal," Duke Senior replied.

"You are speaking to me very gently and hospitably," Orlando said, sheathing his sword. "Pardon me, please. I thought that all things were savage here, and therefore I have acted like a savage. But whoever you are in this hard-to-reach lonely place, who sit under the shade of melancholy boughs and forget and neglect the creeping hours of time, if ever you have looked on better days, if you have ever been where bells have knolled to alert people to go to church, if you have ever sat at any good man's feast, if ever from your eyelids you have wiped a tear and know what it is to pity and be pitied, then let my kindness and nobility persuade you that I am civilized. Now I blush with shame, and I put away my sword."

"It is true that we have seen better days," Duke Senior said, "and we have heard the holy bell knoll to tell us to go to church and we have sat at good men's feasts and wiped our eyes of tears that sacred pity has caused. Therefore, welcome and sit down and take whatever you desire to satisfy your needs."

"For a little while longer, then, refrain from eating," Orlando said. "Wait while I, like a doe, go to find my fawn so I can bring it here and give it food. Nearby is an old poor man, who with me has many weary steps limped in pure love. Until that man — who is oppressed with the two evils of age and hunger — has eaten, I will not touch a bite."

"Go and bring him here," Duke Senior said. "We will not eat until you return."

"Thank you," Orlando said. "May God bless you for your hospitality."

Orlando left to get Adam.

Duke Senior said to Jaques, "You can see that we are not the only ones who are unhappy: This wide and universal theater known as the world presents more woeful pageants than the scene in which we play our parts."

Jaques replied, "All the world is a stage, and all the men and women in it are merely actors: They have their exits and their entrances, and one man in his lifetime plays many parts. His parts are for seven ages.

"First, he plays the infant, mewling and puking in the wet nurse's arms.

"Second, he plays the whining schoolboy with his satchel and shining morning face, creeping like a snail as he unwillingly goes to school.

"Third, he plays the lover, sighing like a furnace breathing out smoke and singing a woeful ballad about his girlfriend's eyebrows.

"Fourth, he plays the soldier, full of strange oaths and bearded like the leopard, fiercely protective of his honor, impetuous and quick in quarrel, facing the mouth of a cannon as he seeks fame, which lasts no longer than a bubble.

"Fifth, he plays the judge, with a fair round belly stuffed with tasty chicken, the bribe of choice, and he plays the part with wise sayings and clichéd examples.

"Sixth, he plays an old man — the lean and slippered and ridiculous pantaloon — wearing spectacles on his nose and a moneybag at his side. The carefully preserved pants that he wore as a young man are now a world too wide for his shrunken legs, and his big manly voice, regressing to a childish treble, squeaks and whistles as he speaks.

"Seventh, and last, he plays the really old man — the part that will end his history — in his second childhood in utter forgetfulness, without teeth, without eyes, without taste, smell, or enjoyment, without everything."

Orlando now returned. He was carrying Adam, an old man of much virtue and loyalty and generosity.

Duke Senior said to Orlando, "Welcome. Set down your venerable burden, and let him eat."

"I thank you most for him," Orlando said.

Adam said weakly to Orlando, "There is need for you to thank him."

He said to Duke Senior, "I scarcely can speak to thank you for myself."

"Welcome," Duke Senior said again. "Fall to. Eat. I will not trouble you now with questions about your fortunes."

He ordered, "Give us some music, and, good Amiens, sing."

Amiens sang, "*Blow, blow, you winter wind.*
"*You are not as unkind*
"*As man's ingratitude;*
"*Your tooth is not as keen,*
"*Because you are not seen,*
"*Although your breath is cruel.*
"*Heigh-ho! Sing heigh-ho to the green holly.*
"*Most friendship is feigning, most loving is mere folly.*
"*So sing heigh-ho to the holly!*
"*This life is most jolly.*
"*Freeze, freeze, you bitter sky,*
"*That does not bite as deeply*
"*As forgotten favors.*
"*Though you turn waters to ice,*
"*Your sting is not so sharp*
"*As the pain of a friend who has forgotten you.*
"*Heigh-ho! Sing heigh-ho to the green holly.*
"*Most friendship is feigning, most loving is mere folly.*
"*So sing heigh-ho to the holly!*
"*This life is most jolly.*"

Suffering can be physical or mental. The mental suffering caused by man's ingratitude is worse than the physical suffering caused by a cold winter wind.

As Amiens sang, Adam and Orlando ate. Orlando also whispered to Duke Senior, who now said, "If you are really the good Sir Rowland's son, as you have whispered to me that you are, and as I can see a strong resemblance to him depicted and living in your face, then be truly welcome here. I am Duke Senior, and I truly respected your father. We will now go into my cave and you can tell me the rest of your story."

To Adam, he said, "Good old man, you are as welcome as your master is."

To Orlando, he said, "Support him by the arm."

To Adam, he said, "Give me your hand."

To both Orlando and Adam, he said, "Now I want to hear about your histories and adventures."

CHAPTER 3

— 3.1 —

In a room of his palace, Duke Frederick was questioning Oliver. Some other Lords were present.

Duke Frederick said to Oliver, "You have not seen him since the wrestling match? Sir, sir, that is not possible. If I were not for the most part made of mercy, I would not seek Orlando since I have you here to take the brunt of my revenge. But note well: Find your brother, wherever he is. Seek him diligently, with candle if need be, like the parable in Luke 15:8-10 about the woman who lost a silver coin, lit a candle, and searched for the coin until she found it. Bring your brother back here dead or alive within the next twelve months, or return no more to seek a living in our territory. All of your lands and all of the things worth seizure that you call yours we now seize into our hands. We will keep them until you return with your brother and use his testimony to acquit yourself of the crimes of which we think you are guilty."

"I wish that your highness knew my thoughts and feelings," Oliver said. "I have never loved my brother in my life."

"Then you are even more of a villain than I thought," Duke Frederick said, ignoring the way that he had treated his own brother: Duke Senior.

To the others, he said, "Throw Oliver out of the palace; my officers will seize his house and lands. Do this quickly and send him on his way."

— 3.2 —

In the Forest of Arden, Orlando hung a love poem on a tree and said, "Hang there, my verse, as a witness of my love, and you, thrice-crowned goddess and queen of night — crowned once as the Moon goddess Luna, a second time as Diana on Earth, and a third time as Proserpina, aka Persephone, in the Underworld — look with your chaste eye, from your pale sphere above, upon Rosalind, who is a virgin like yourself. Because she is a virgin, she is one of your followers. She, your follower, rules my life. Rosalind! These trees shall be my books and in their bark I will write my thoughts so that every eye that looks in this forest shall see testaments to your excellence everywhere. Run, run, Orlando — carve on every tree testaments to the beautiful, virginal, and indescribable she."

Orlando ran.

Nearby, the old shepherd Corin and the professional jester Touchstone were talking.

Corin asked Touchstone, "And how do you like this shepherd's life, Mr. Touchstone?"

"Truly, shepherd, in itself, it is a good life, but because it is a shepherd's life, it is a bad life. Because it is solitary, I like it very well; but because it is lonely, I don't like it at all. Now, because it is in the fields, it pleases me well; but because it is not in the court, it is boring and does not please me. Because it is a simple life, it suits me well, but because there is no more plenty in it, it goes much against my stomach and does not suit me. Do you have any philosophy in you, shepherd?"

"No more but that I know the more one sickens the worse at ease he is," Corin said, "and I know that a man who lacks money, resources, and happiness is without three good friends. I know that the property of rain is to be wet and the property of fire is to burn, that good pasture makes fat sheep, and that a great cause of the night is lack of the Sun, and that a man who has acquired no intelligence either by birth or education may complain that he lacks a good upbringing or that he comes from a stupid family."

"Such a man as yourself is a natural philosopher," Touchstone said. "Have you ever been at court, shepherd?"

"No, indeed."

"Then you are damned," Touchstone said.

"I hope not."

Touchstone was joking, as jesters so often do, and Corin knew it.

"Indeed, you are damned like an ill-roasted egg, all on one side."

Corin knew about roasting eggs in ashes. They needed to be turned, or they would roast only on one side.

"I am damned like an ill-roasted egg for not being at court? Explain why you think that."

"If you have never been at court, then you have never seen good manners. If you have never seen good manners, then your manners are wicked. Wickedness is sin, and sin results in damnation. You are in a dangerous position, shepherd."

"Not at all, Touchstone," Corin replied. "The good manners that are suitable for the court are as ridiculous in the country as the behavior of the country folk is most mockable at the court. You told me that you do not greet each other at the court without kissing each other's hands. That custom would be unhygienic, if courtiers were shepherds."

"Explain your reasoning. Quickly, explain your reasoning."

"We are always handling our ewes, and their fleeces, as you know, are greasy."

"Why, the hands of courtiers also sweat. The grease of an ewe is as wholesome as the sweat of a man. You have not made a good argument. Therefore, make a better one."

"In addition to that, our hands are hard."

"Your lips will feel them the sooner when you kiss them, and so you do not need kiss very long. Come up with a better argument."

"We use tar when treating the injuries of our sheep, and so tar is often on our hands. Would you have us kiss tar? In contrast, the hands of the courtier are perfumed."

"You shallow thinker! Compared to a good steak, you are a piece of flesh covered with maggots. Learn of the wise, and perpend. Perfume has a base of civet, which is the secretion from the anal glands of a civet cat. Tar is a cleaner substance than civit. Can you come up with a better argument?"

"You have too courtly a wit for me. I give up."

"Will you give up, still damned?" Touchstone joked. "God help you, shallow man! May God make an incision in you and let the bad blood and damnation out. You are ill."

"Sir, I am a trustworthy laborer," Corin said. "I earn what I eat, earn what I wear, owe no man hate, envy no man's happiness, am glad of other men's good luck and lives, resigned to any afflictions I face, and my greatest pride is to see my ewes graze and my lambs suck."

"That is another foolish sin in you: you bring the ewes and the rams together and attempt to get your living by the copulation of animals. You act as a pimp to the leading sheep of the flock and you betray a she-lamb only a year old by breeding her to a crooked-horned, old, possessed-of-an-unfaithful-ewe ram — that is an unreasonable and unethical match of female and male. If you are not damned for this, the Devil himself will not allow such evil beings as shepherds to enter his Hell — I cannot see any other way that you can escape Hell."

Corin said to Touchstone, "Look, here comes young Master Ganymede, the brother of my new female employer, Aliena."

Rosalind walked toward them. She was reading one of the love poems that Orlando had tied to trees.

Rosalind read out loud this poem:

"*From the East Indies to the West Indies,*
"*There is no jewel like Rosalind.*
"*Her worth, being mounted on the wind,*
"*Through all the world bears Rosalind.*
"*All the pictures fairest sketched and lined*
"*Are but black compared to Rosalind.*
"*Let no fair be kept in mind*
"*But the fair face of Rosalind.*"

Touchstone knew that this was bad poetry. He said to Rosalind, who as usual was dressed in men's clothing and going by the name Ganymede, "Writing good poetry is difficult; writing bad poetry is easy. I can rhyme you poetry like that for eight years without stopping, except for dinners and suppers and sleeping-hours. That kind of poetry jogs along like dairy women bumpily riding to the market."

Bad poetry or not, it was love poetry about her, so Rosalind said, "Be quiet, fool!"

Touchstone was not quiet. He said, "Here's an example of the bad poetry I will write:

"If a male deer — a hart — do lack a female deer — a hind,

"Let him seek out Rosalind.

"If the cat will seek its own kind,

"So be sure will Rosalind.

"Winter garments must be stuffed with padding — that is, lined,

"And stuffed must be slender Rosalind.

"They who reap must make sheaves and them bind;

"Then put them on a cart with Rosalind."

Rosalind smiled. She knew that prostitutes were placed on a cart to be taken to prison. She also knew what kind of stuffing of a young woman Touchstone was referring to.

Touchstone continued his bad poetry:

"The sweetest nut has the sourest rind,

"Such a nut is Rosalind.

"He that sweetest rose will find

"Must find love's prick and so will Rosalind."

Rosalind smiled again. She knew that "prick" had a double meaning.

Touchstone said about the bad poetry that Rosalind had been reading, "This is the very false gallop of unmetrical verses. Why do you infect yourself with them?"

"Be quiet, you dull fool! I found them on a tree."

"Truly, the tree yields bad fruit."

"I will graft the tree with you, and then I will graft it with a medlar branch. Then the tree will bear the earliest fruit in the country — you will be rotten before you are half ripe, and that is the true quality of the medlar. The medlar is not ripe enough to eat until it is rotten. This is an appropriate comparison because you are a meddler."

"You have spoken, but whether you have spoken wisely, we will let the forest judge."

Celia had found one of the poems that Orlando had written and then tied to a tree. She walked toward Rosalind and Touchstone. She did not see them because her eyes looked down as she read the poem.

Rosalind said, "Be quiet, Touchstone!"

Keeping in character as Ganymede, a wise thing to do to prevent mistakes that could reveal her secret identity, she said, "Here comes my sister, reading. Let's stand aside and spy on her."

Celia read out loud, "*Why should this a desert be?*
"*Because it is unpeopled? No:*
"*Tongues I'll hang on every tree,*
"*That shall civil sayings show:*
"*Some, how brief the life of man*
"*Runs his erring pilgrimage,*
"*That the stretching of the span of a hand*
"*Limits his sum of age;*
"*Some, of violated vows*
"*Between the souls of friend and friend:*
"*But upon the fairest boughs,*
"*Or at every sentence's end,*
"*Will I 'Rosalinda' write,*
"*Teaching all who read to know*
"*The quintessence of every soul*
"*Heaven would in miniature show.*
"*Therefore Heaven Nature charged*
"*That one body should be filled*
"*With all graces wide-enlarged:*
"*Nature presently distilled*
"*Helen's cheek, but not her heart,*
"*Cleopatra's majesty,*
"*Atalanta's better part,*
"*Sad Lucretia's modesty.*
"*Thus Rosalind of many parts*
"*By Heavenly council was devised,*
"*Of many faces, eyes, and hearts,*
"*To have the features dearest prized.*

"Heaven decreed that she these gifts should have,

"And I to live and die her slave."

The poem may have been badly written, but it was complimentary to Rosalind: Heavenly beings had conspired to give her the best qualities of ancient heroines. According to the author of the poem, the Heavenly beings had given Rosalind the beauty of Helen of Troy but not her character — Helen had deserted her daughter and husband and had run away with Paris, Prince of Troy.

The Heavenly beings also had given Rosalind the majesty of Cleopatra, Queen of Egypt.

The Heavenly beings also had given Rosalind the "better part" of Atalanta, who wished to preserve her chastity. Being swift, she challenged her suitors to a foot race. If she won the foot race, she would remain unmarried. If a suitor won the footrace, she would marry that suitor. For a long time, she remained a virgin, but Venus, the goddess of sexual passion, helped Hippomenes to win the foot race. She gave him three golden apples, and during the foot race, he dropped the golden apples, one at a time. Atalanta picked up the golden apples, and this slowed her down enough that Hippomenes won the race and married her. Fortunately, Rosalind did not get the worse part of Atalanta: her cruelty. All the suitors who lost the footrace were killed.

The Heavenly beings also had given Rosalind the modesty of Lucretia, who committed suicide after being raped by Sextus Tarquinius, the son of the Etruscan King: Lucius Tarquinius Superbus. The Romans then threw out the Etruscan King and started the Roman Republic.

Rosalind and Touchstone now came out of hiding. Rosalind startled Celia by exclaiming, "Oh, preacher. With what tedious homilies about love have you been wearing out your parishioners? You should have warned them in advance: 'You will need great patience to listen to this!'"

"You are false friends for spying on me," Celia joked. Then she said to Corin, "Shepherd, go away a little so that we can have some privacy."

Because she wanted to engage in girl talk with Rosalind, she said to Touchstone, "Go with him."

Touchstone said, "Come, shepherd, let us make an honorable retreat. We may not be with bag and baggage, yet we will have my scrip — my pouch — and scrippage — the coins I put in it."

As Corin and Touchstone walked away, both Rosalind and Celia smiled. They knew that "bag and baggage" referred to the military equipment that could be taken away by soldiers as they retreated. They also knew that "bag and baggage" were less-than-complimentary terms when applied to women. A "bag" is an unattractive or elderly woman. "Baggage" is a woman of immoral life — a strumpet. "Baggage" can also be used playfully to describe a cunning or saucy young woman. They also knew that professional jesters have the freedom to use such terms. In return, the jesters' victims were allowed to freely call the jester a fool, a term that was not exactly an insult.

Celia asked Rosalind, "Did you hear these verses?"

"Oh, yes, I heard them all, and more, too; for some of the verses had more feet than the verses could bear or carry."

"That doesn't matter. The feet should bear the verses."

"True, but these feet were lame and could not bear themselves outside the verse and therefore stood lamely in the verse."

Celia asked, "Did you hear these poems without wondering how it came to pass that your name is written in the bark of trees and poems about you are hung in the trees?"

"If this is a nine-days'-wonder, I had experienced seven of the nine days before you came here just now. Look at this poem: I found it on a palm-tree. I was never so be-rhymed since Pythagoras' time, when I was an Irish rat, which I can hardly remember. Pythagoras thought that souls could be reincarnated in the bodies of animals, and the Irish thought that they could rid themselves of rats with the use of rhyming incantations."

"Can you guess who wrote these poems and carved your name into the bark of trees?"

"Is it a man?" Rosalind joked.

"Yes, and he wears a necklace around his neck — a necklace that you once gave him."

Celia asked, "Are you blushing?"

Rosalind knew that the man had to be Orlando, but she wanted Celia to say his name.

"Please tell me. What is the man's name?"

"Lord, it is difficult for friends to meet, but mountains can be moved by earthquakes and so meet. This is true even though people usually think that friends may meet, but mountains never greet. You already know the answer, don't you?"

"No," Rosalind lied. "Who is it?"

"Is it possible that you don't know?"

"I don't know. Please, I urgently ask you to tell me who he is who wrote the poems."

"Oh, wonderful, wonderful, and most wonderful wonderful — and yet again wonderful, and after that, wonderful beyond all words!"

"Celia, please! Do you think that because I am dressed like a man that I am a man in my disposition! One inch of delay more is like the distance it would take to journey to the South Seas on an expedition of discovery. Please, tell me immediately what I want to know! Who wrote those poems! Speak up, and speak up quickly! I wish that you could stammer, so that you could pour this mystery man out of your mouth the way that wine comes out of a narrow-mouthed bottle: either too much at once, or none at all. These, of course, alternate, and I would eventually learn the name that I want to know. Please, take the cork out of your mouth so that I can drink your news. Stop teasing me, and pour out the name that I want to know."

"You want to know the name so that you can put a man in your belly."

Rosalind thought, *Celia is referring either to my being pregnant with a son or to the act that could result in my being pregnant with a son. But yes, I want her to name the name of Orlando, whom I want to father my children.*

She asked, "Is he a normal man and made by God? What manner of man is he? Is his head worth a hat? Is his chin worth a beard?"

"He has only a little beard."

"Well, God will send him more beard, if the man will be thankful. I can wait for the growth of his beard if you will now tell me on whose chin it will grow."

Finally, Celia stopped teasing Rosalind and gave her the answer that she had hoped and expected to hear: "It is young Orlando, who conquered the wrestler and your heart both in an instant."

Happy, Rosalind said, "May the Devil take you if you are lying. Speak truthfully, serious and honest maiden."

"Truly, he is Orlando."

"Orlando?"

"Orlando."

Rosalind was delighted, but she was in disguise and dressed as a young man — something that could interfere with Orlando's wooing of her. She said, "What shall I do with my man's jacket and trousers?"

She then inundated Celia with questions: "What was he doing when you saw him? What did he say? How did he look? How was he dressed? What is he doing here? Did he ask about me? Where is he now? What happened when he departed from you? And when shall you see him again? Answer me in one word."

"To answer all those questions in one word, I would need the large mouth of Rabelais' comic creation: the giant Gargantua. Such a quantity of all-run-together syllables is too large for any normal-sized mouth. To say yes and no to your questions is more time-consuming than to answer the questions of a religious catechism."

"Does Orlando know that I am in this forest and that I am wearing men's clothing? Does he look as healthy as he did the day he wrestled?"

"Counting the specks of dust in a ray of Sunshine is as easy as answering the questions of a lover, but I will tell you where I saw him. Pay attention. I found him under a tree, like a dropped acorn."

"The oak is known as the tree of Jupiter, as well it should be known, since it drops such fruit."

"Please listen, good madam."

"Proceed."

"There he lay, stretched along the ground, like a wounded knight."

"Though it would be a pity to see such a sight, such a figure well becomes the ground."

"Cry 'whoa!' to your tongue, please. It prances along in an ill-timed manner. He was dressed and equipped like a hunter hunting a male deer: a hart."

"This is ominous," Rosalind said. "He comes here to kill my heart."

"I would like to sing my song without accompaniment. You are making me sing out of tune."

"Don't you know that I am a woman? What I think, I must speak. Sweetie, speak on."

"You are making me forget which words to use — but look! Isn't that him coming this way?"

Rosalind looked up and saw Orlando and Jaques walking together. She said, "Yes, it is him. Let us hide and spy on him."

Orlando and Jaques had met in the forest. Now they were humorously and courteously insulting each other.

"I thank you for your company," Jaques said, "but, to be honest, I would have preferred to be alone."

"As had I," Orlando replied, "but, because it is good manners, I also thank you for your company."

"May God be with you, and may the two of us meet as seldom as we can."

"I do desire that we may become better strangers."

"Please, mar no more trees by writing names on their bark and hanging love poems from their branches."

"Please, mar no more of my verses by reading them badly."

"Is Rosalind your love's name?"

"Yes, exactly."

"I do not like her name."

"There was no thought of pleasing you when she was given a Christian name at her baptism."

"How tall is she?"

"She stands just as high as my heart."

"You are full of pretty answers. You must know some goldsmiths' wives — you must have learned your pretty answers by memorizing the inscriptions on the inside of rings."

Jaques thought, *"She stands just as high as my heart." Good grief!*

"That is not so," Orlando said, "but I am answering your questions, which you seem to have learned from those on inspirational and religious posters."

"You have a nimble wit. I think it was made from the swift heels of the swift runner Atalanta. Will you sit down with me? We two shall rail against our mistress the world and all our misery."

"I will criticize no living person in the world but myself, whose faults I know best."

"The worst fault you have is being in love," Jaques said.

"It is a fault that I will not exchange for your best virtue. I am weary of you."

"To tell the truth, I was looking for a fool when I found you."

"He is drowned in the brook. Look in the brook, and you shall see him."

"There I shall see my own reflection."

"In my opinion, that which would be reflected is either a fool or nothing."

"I will stay no more with you. Farewell, Mr. Love."

"I am glad that you are leaving. Adieu, good Monsieur Melancholy."

Jaques walked away, and Rosalind whispered to Celia, "I will speak to Orlando like a saucy lackey and trick him while I pretend to be a young man."

Rosalind said to Orlando, "How are you, forester?"

"Very well. What do you want?"

"Please, what o'clock is it?"

"You should ask me about the time of day in more general terms — there is no clock in the forest and so I can't be specific."

"Then there is no true lover in the forest," Rosalind, dressed as Ganymede, said. "If there were a true lover in the forest, we would be able to tell the exact time by counting the number of the lover's sighs per minute and the number of the lover's groans per hour. That would tell the lazy passage of Time."

"Why not the swift passage of Time? Wouldn't the lover's sighs and groans tell that?"

"Not at all, sir," Rosalind replied. "Time passes differently for different kinds of people. For some people, Time ambles pleasurably. For some people, Time trots hard. For some people, Time gallops quickly. For some people, Time stands still."

"For whom does Time trot hard?"

"Time trots hard and violently for a young maiden between the day of her engagement and the day of her marriage. Even if that time is a week, time trots so hard that it seems like seven years."

"For whom does Time amble pleasurably?"

"Time ambles pleasurably for a priest who does not know Latin and a rich man who does not have the gout. The priest sleeps easily because he cannot study the Bible and other religious works, all of which are in the language of the learned: Latin. Therefore, he lacks the burden of hard study that makes him waste away. The rich man lives merrily because he feels no pain and knows no burden of heavy and painful poverty. For these men, Time ambles pleasurably."

"For whom does Time gallop quickly?"

"Time gallops quickly for a thief on his way to the gallows. Although he goes as slowly as he can, he thinks that he gets there too quickly."

"For whom does Time stand still?"

"Time stands still for lawyers during the period when the law courts are not in session. The lawyers sleep and do not see Time passing."

"Where do you live, pretty youth?" Orlando asked.

"I live with this shepherdess, my sister, here in the outskirts of the forest, like fringe upon a petticoat."

"Were you born here?"

"Yes, just like a rabbit that lives where it was born."

"Your speech is more citified than it should be in so remote a dwelling."

"I have been told that by many people," Rosalind replied, "but indeed an old religious uncle of mine taught me to speak; in his youth, he lived in a city. I am citified enough to be interested in what o'clock it is. He understood courtship too well because in the city he fell in love. I have heard him read many lectures against it, and I thank God that I am not a woman who is afflicted with all the many giddy offences of which he says women are guilty."

"Can you remember any of the principal evils that he claimed that women are guilty of?"

"There were none that really stood out. They were all similar to one another the way that halfpence, which have similar markings, are. Every fault seemed monstrous until its fellow fault came to match it."

"Please, tell me about some of them."

"No, I will not give away my medicine to anyone except those who are sick. There is a man who haunts the forest, who abuses our young trees by carving 'Rosalind' on their bark. He hangs odes upon hawthorns and elegies upon brambles. All of these deify the name of Rosalind. If I could meet that fancy-monger, I would give him some good counsel, for he seems to have the sickness of love upon him."

"I am he who is so shaken by lovesickness. Please tell me your remedy for my lovesickness."

"You have none of the marks of lovesickness that my uncle taught me. He taught me how to know when a man is in love. I am sure that you are not a prisoner in that flimsy cage of rushes. You are not a prisoner of love."

"What are the marks of lovesickness that your uncle taught you?"

"They were a lean cheek, which you have not; dark circles under the eyes, which you have not; an impatient spirit, which you have not; a neglected beard, which you have not, but I pardon you for that because you have little beard — your beard is as big as a younger brother's revenue. Other marks were that your stockings should be ungartered, your hat should be without a band, your sleeve unbuttoned, your shoes untied, and everything about you demonstrating a desperate neglect of how you are dressed. But you are no such man: You are meticulous in your apparel, and you seem to love yourself more than you love someone else."

"Fair youth, I wish I could make you believe that I am in love."

"Make me believe it! You may sooner make the woman whom you love believe it. I think that she is apter to believe than to admit that she does believe it. That is one of the ways in which women lie about their real feelings. But are you truly the man who hangs the verses on the trees — the verses wherein Rosalind is so praised and admired?"

"I swear to you, youth, by the white hand of Rosalind, I am that man, that unfortunate man."

"But are you as much in love as your rhymes say that you are?"

"Neither rhyme nor reason can express how much I am in love with Rosalind."

"Love is merely a madness, and, I tell you, lovers deserve to be treated the way that madmen are — kept in a dark house and whipped to get the demon that causes their madness out of them. The reason that lovers are not punished in that way and cured of their lovesickness is that the madness is so common that the whippers are in love, too. Yet I am an expert in curing lovesickness through my advice."

"Have you ever cured anyone of lovesickness?"

"Yes, one person, and in this manner. He pretended that I was his loved one, and I made him pretend everyday to woo me, at which time I would, being but a Moonish — that is, changeable and fickle — youth myself, be sad, effeminate, changeable, longing and liking, proud, capricious, affected, shallow, inconstant, full of tears, and full of smiles. I acted as if I felt every emotion or as if I felt no emotion. I acted one way, and then I acted the opposite way. Both boys and women are for the most part creatures of this color: changeable and fickle. I would like him, and then I would loathe him. I would entertain him, and then I would forswear him. I would weep for him, and then I would spit at him. By acting in this way, I drove lovesickness out of my suitor and I delivered to him another kind of madness: He renounced the world, and he decided to live in complete religious seclusion. In this way, I cured him, and I am willing to cure you in the same way — I will wash your heart and make it as clean as a sound sheep's heart — there will not be one spot of love in your heart."

"I don't want to be cured of my lovesickness, youth."

"I will cure you, if you will call me Rosalind and come everyday to my cottage and woo me."

"I have such faith in my love for Rosalind that I accept your challenge — you will not be able to cure me of my love for her," Orlando said. "Now tell me where your cottage is."

"Come with me and I will show you where it is. While we walk, you can tell me where in the forest you live. Will you come with me?"

"With all my heart, good youth."

"You must call me Rosalind."

She asked Celia, "Come, sister, will you go with us?"

Rosalind thought, *My meetings with Orlando will work out well. He needs to talk to me, not write poetry about me.*

— 3.3 —

In another part of the forest, Touchstone was talking to Audrey, a goatherd. Jaques was close enough to them to overhear what they said.

"Come quickly, good Audrey. I will help you with your goats, Audrey. And what do you think, Audrey? Am I the man for you? Do the simple features of my face content you?"

"Your features!" Audrey said. "Lord help us! What features!"

"I am here with you and your goats, just like the most capricious of the Roman poets, honest Ovid, was among the Goths."

Touchstone knew that Audrey had never heard of Ovid, author of *Metamorphoses*.

Jaques enjoyed watching Touchstone court Audrey: A well-educated man was courting an ill-educated young woman. Jaques said to himself, "Touchstone's knowledge is being put to ill use. His company cannot appreciate his intelligence and education. This is worse than the god Jupiter coming down from Mount Olympus to spend time as the guest of peasants in a thatched cottage."

Touchstone said, "When a man's verses cannot be understood, and when a man's good jokes are not understood, it metaphorically kills a man just like an argument over a big bill for a short visit in a small room. But I doubt that forest-dwelling people have heard that the great playwright Christopher Marlowe was killed in an argument about a big bill. Truly, Audrey, I wish that the gods had made you poetical."

"I do not know what the word 'poetical' means. Does it mean being respectable in deed and word? Does it mean being truthful?"

"No, indeed. The truest poetry is the most feigning — the most imaginative. Lovers are fond of poetry, and what lovers swear in poetry may be said to be lies."

"Do you wish then that the gods had made me poetical?"

"I do, truly. You have sworn to me that you are chaste. If you were a poet, I could hope that you were lying."

"Don't you want me to be chaste?" Audrey asked.

"No, indeed, unless you were ugly. Chastity and beauty are like honey and sugar — two things that when they go together are too sweet. No one needs to pour honey on sugar."

Jaques said to himself, "This fool sometimes makes sense."

Touchstone thought, *When a woman is beautiful, I hope that she is not chaste so that I may sleep with her without having to marry her.*

"Well, I am not beautiful," Audrey said, "and therefore I pray that the gods will make me chaste."

"Indeed, you should wish that you be chaste. Wasting chastity on a dirty slut is like putting good meat on a dirty dish."

"I am not a slut, though I thank the gods I am ugly."

"Well, praised be the gods that you are ugly! Sluttishness may come hereafter. But be it as it may be, I want to marry you, and to that end I have met with Sir Oliver Martext, the vicar of the nearby village, who has promised to meet me here and to marry us."

"I would like to see this meeting," Jaques said to himself.

"I agree to marry you," Audrey said. "May the gods give us joy!"

"Amen," Touchstone said. "A man could, if he had a fearful heart, hesitate about getting married here because here we have no church but the forest, no congregation but horned beasts. That could make a man afraid that the horns were an evil omen. Horns are the symbol of a cuckold — a man with an unfaithful wife. But what of that! Have courage, Touchstone! Horns may be odious, but they are inevitable. It is said, 'Many a man thinks that his wealth is exhaustible.' That is true: Many men have horns and will never see the end of the horns that his wife gives him. Well, horns are the dowry that having a wife gets him. The husband does not get his own horns. Horns? Definitely they exist. Do only poor men get horns? No, no; the noblest stag has horns as big as the horns of the rascal. Is the single man therefore blessed because he lacks horns? No.

"A town with a wall is better off than a village without a wall, and so a married man with horns is better off than a bachelor without horns. The horns protect the man's head like the walls protect the town. It is better to know the art of defense than not to know it, and it is better to get horns than to have no sex at all. To say the truth, a wife is worth defending."

He paused, and then said, "Here comes Sir Oliver Martext, the vicar of the next village."

Touchstone said, "Sir Oliver Martext, we are happy to see you. Will you marry us here under this tree, or shall we go with you to your chapel?"

"Is there anyone here to give away the woman?"

"I will not take her as the gift of any man. I don't want sloppy seconds," Touchstone said.

"Truly, she must be given away, or the marriage is not lawful."

Jaques came forward and said, "Proceed with the wedding. I will give her away."

Touchstone said to Jaques, "Good day, good Master What-do-ye-call-it."

Jaques knew that Touchstone was pretending not to want to say "Jaques" in front of the priest — one way to pronounce "Jaques" is "Jakes," a word meaning "toilet."

Touchstone continued, "How do you do, sir? It is good to see you. I enjoyed talking to you the last time we met. I am very glad to see you. We have a little ceremony taking place here."

Touchstone added, "You may keep your head covered. Keep your hat on your head. No one is here to whom you need show that much respect."

"Will you be married today, motley fool?" Jaques asked.

"The ox has a yoke, sir. The horse has a bridle. The falcon has bells attached to its feet in order to make it easier to find. Men have sexual desires that need to be in some way controlled. Pigeons stroke their beaks together, and marriage allows men and women to kiss — and more."

"And will you, a man of good breeding, be married under a bush like a beggar?" Jaques asked. "Go to a church, and have a good priest who can tell you what marriage is. This Sir Oliver fellow will only join you together as they join together the sections of wood paneling on walls. One of you will turn out to be a bad panel and like green timber over time will warp, and the two of you will be pulled apart."

Touchstone said, "Perhaps I will be better off married by Sir Oliver than by another priest. He is not likely to marry me properly, and if I am not married properly, I will have a good excuse later to leave my wife."

"Come with me," Jaques said, "and let me give you advice."

Touchstone said, "Come with me, sweet Audrey. We must get married, or we will live in bawdry."

He added, "Farewell, good Master Oliver. Let us not sing this popular song:

"*Oh, sweet Oliver,*

"*Oh, handsome Oliver,*

"*Don't leave me behind.'*

"Instead, let us sing this song:

"*Go away quickly,*

"*Begone, I say,*

"*I will not go to the wedding with you.'"*

Jaques, Touchstone, and Audrey left, leaving Sir Oliver behind, who said, "It does not matter that no wedding was performed. None of these capricious rascals will succeed in mocking me enough to drive me away from pursuing my calling."

— 3.4 —

In another part of the forest, Rosalind and Celia were talking. Rosalind was upset because Oliver had not come to woo her at the time they had arranged.

"Don't talk to me," Rosalind said. "I am going to cry."

"If you want to cry, then cry. But remember that tears do not become a man."

"Don't I have a good reason to cry?"

"You have as good a reason as anyone to cry, so therefore cry."

"Orlando's red hair is the same color as the hair of Judas, who betrayed Christ with a kiss."

"I think that his hair is somewhat browner than the hair of Judas, but his kisses are like those of Judas."

"Actually, his hair is a good color," Rosalind said.

"His hair is an excellent color," Celia said, humoring her friend. "Chestnut is the very best color."

"And his kisses are as full of saintliness as the touch of holy bread — bread blessed in the church and then distributed to the poor."

"He has acquired a pair of the cast-off, cast-iron, chaste lips from a statue-in-progress of Diana, goddess of virginity. Not even a nun who has pledged herself to a life of cold and barren chastity kisses with greater purity. The very ice of chastity is in his kisses."

"But why did he swear that he would come this morning, and he has not come?"

"To be certain, there is no truth in him."

"Do you think so?"

"Yes. I do not think that he is a pick-pocket or a horse-thief, but as for his truthfulness in love, I think that his promises are like an empty goblet or a hollow, worm-eaten nut."

"You do not think that he is trustworthy in love?"

"If he were in love, he would be trustworthy, but I do not think that he is in love."

"You have heard him swear plainly that he was."

"'Was' is not 'is,'" Celia said. "Besides, the oath of a lover is no stronger than the word of a tavern owner who overcharges and swears that the bill is accurate. Both of them lie."

She added, "Orlando is staying here in the forest with your father, Duke Senior."

Rosalind said, "I met my father the Duke yesterday and talked to him. Because I am in disguise and because it has been many years since he last saw me, he did not recognize me. He asked about my parents, and I said that they were as good as he was. He laughed and stopped asking me about them. But why are we talking about fathers, when we could be talking about a man such as Orlando?"

"Orlando is an excellent man!" Celia said. "He writes excellent verse, speaks excellent words, swears excellent oaths and breaks them excellently on the heart of his lover, the way that an inexperienced jouster, who spurs his horse on only one side, breaks his staff across the shield of his opponent rather than directly upon the shield. Both Orlando and the novice jouster are notable fools, but everything is excellent when one is young and foolish."

Celia looked up and said, "Who is coming here?"

Corin walked up to Rosalind and Celia and said, "Both of you have often asked about the young shepherd who laments being in love, whom you saw sitting by me on the ground, praising the proud disdainful shepherdess whom he loved."

"Well, what about him?" Celia asked.

"If you want to see a pageant truly played between two opposites — one with the pale complexion of true love and the other with the red glow of scorn and proud disdain — go with me a little distance and I will show it to you."

"Come, let's go with Corin," Rosalind said. "The sight of lovers feeds those in love."

She said to Corin, "Bring us to this sight, and you will be able to say that I proved to be a busy actor in their play."

— 3.5 —

In a nearby part of the forest, the young shepherd Silvius was pleading with his beloved, Phoebe, who did not love him.

Silvius said, "Sweet Phoebe, do not scorn me. Do not, Phoebe. Say that you do not love me, but do not say it so bitterly. The common executioner, whose heart is hard because it is accustomed to death, says 'Forgive me' before he drops his ax on the criminal's neck. Will you be crueler than an executioner who dies and lives by drops of blood?"

Rosalind, Celia, and Corin arrived and witnessed the rest of the scene between the two lovers.

Phoebe replied, "I don't want to be your executioner. I run away from you because I don't want to injure you. You tell me that murder is in my eye. That is very clever of you: It is certain, and very probable — ha! — that eyes, which are the frailest and softest things and which shut their coward gates — their eyelids — against the assaults of specks of dust, ought to be called tyrants, butchers, murderers! Now I am frowning on you with all my heart. If my eyes can wound, now let them kill you. Go ahead and pretend to faint. Go ahead and fall down now. If you cannot, then out of shame stop lying that my eyes are murderers! Go ahead and show me the wound that my eye has made in you. If you scratch yourself with a pin, some mark will remain behind. If you put your hand on some rush plants and lean on them, your palm will bear a mark and indentation for a short while. But my eyes, which I have been darting at you, have not hurt you. I am sure that eyes have no force that can harm anyone."

"Oh, dear Phoebe, if you ever — and that may be soon — meet someone young and handsome who makes you fall in love, then you shall understand the invisible wounds the sharp arrows of love make."

"Until that time, do not come near me. And when that time comes, go ahead and mock me. Do not pity me then because until that time comes I will not pity you."

Rosalind had promised to be a busy actor in their play, and now she came forth and said to Phoebe, "And why won't you pity this young man, I ask you? Who is your mother? Who taught you to insult and exult, both at the same time, over the wretched? You have no beauty — to go to bed in the dark, you must carry a candle, unlike a beautiful woman whose beauty lights up the darkness. So why are you proud and pitiless?"

Phoebe stared at Ganymede. She had fallen in love at first sight with Rosalind, whom she thought to be a young man.

Rosalind noticed Phoebe staring at her and asked, "Why, what do you mean by this? Why are you staring at me?"

Amused, she realized that Phoebe had fallen in love with her. She said to Phoebe, "I see no more in you than in the ordinary ready-made — not specially made — goods for sale in the market. By God, I think you mean to ensnare my eyes, too, and make me love you the way that this young shepherd loves you! No, proud mistress, do not hope that I will fall in love with you. Your inky and ugly brows, your black and ugly silk hair, your black, beady, ugly eyes, and your yellowish-white complexion will not subdue me and make me adore you."

Rosalind said to Silvius, "You foolish shepherd, why do you follow her like the foggy south wind puffing with sighs and tears? You are a thousand times better looking than this woman is. It is such fools as you who fill the world full of ugly children after you marry ugly women. It is not her mirror that flatters her — you do. With you serving as her mirror, she sees herself looking more beautiful than the features of her face justify."

Rosalind said to Phoebe, "Young woman, know yourself: Get down on your knees and fast and thank heaven for this good man's love: For I must tell you as a friend in your ear, 'Sell when you can: you are not for all markets. Get a man while you can. You are not pretty enough to get many offers.' Beg this man to forgive you, and take his offer. Foul is most foul, being foul to be a scoffer — ugliness is at its most ugly when it is combined with scornfulness."

Phoebe replied, "Sweet youth, please criticize me for a year without stopping. I prefer to hear you criticize me than to hear this man woo me."

"Silvius has fallen in love with your scornfulness," Rosalind said to Phoebe.

"And now Phoebe is falling in love with my anger," Rosalind said to Celia and Corin.

To Silvius, Rosalind said, "If this is true, as quickly as she answers you with frowns, I'll rebuke her sharply with bitter words."

She asked Phoebe, "Why are you looking at me like that?"

"I bear you no ill will."

"Please, do not fall in love with me," Rosalind said. "I am falser than vows made when drunk. Besides, I don't like you."

Rosalind said to Silvius, "If you want to know where I live, my cottage is in that grove of olive trees over there."

She asked Celia, "Will you go with me now, sister?"

She advised Silvius, "Shepherd, woo Phoebe vigorously."

She said to Celia, "Come, sister."

She advised Phoebe, "Shepherdess, look more favorably on Silvius, and do not be proud. Even if everyone in the world could see you, he is the only man who would find you attractive."

She said to Celia and Corin, "Come, let us return to our flock."

Rosalind, Celia, and Corin departed, and Phoebe said to herself, "Dead Shepherd, dear Christopher Marlowe, now I understand what you meant when you wrote, 'Who ever loved that loved not at first sight?'"

Silvius began, "Sweet Phoebe —"

Phoebe asked, "What do you want, Silvius?"

Silvius said, "Sweet Phoebe, pity me."

"Why, I am sorry for you, gentle Silvius."

"Wherever sorrow is, relief should be. If you feel sorrow at my grief in love, you should give me your love. That way, both your sorrow and my grief would be exterminated."

"You have my love. Is not that neighborly? Christ said in Mark 12:31, 'Thou shalt love thy neighbor as thyself.'"

Silvius said, "That is not the kind of love I want. I want you."

"Why, that is covetousness. The Bible says in Exodus 20:17, 'Thou shalt not covet thy neighbor's house, thou shalt not covet thy neighbor's wife, nor his manservant, nor his maidservant, nor his ox, nor his ass, nor any thing that is thy neighbor's.'"

She thought to herself, *I have given my heart to that young man — the neighbor of Silvius — who criticized me. Silvius is coveting something that belongs to his neighbor.*

She added, "Silvius, I have hated you, but now I will endure your company, which previously was irksome to me. I am doing this not because I love you, but because you can talk about love so well. I also have an errand for you, but you must not ask for anything more than your own happiness that I find you useful."

Silvius replied, "So holy and so perfect is my love for you and I am so lacking in your favor that I will think it a most plenteous crop to glean the leftover and broken ears of corn after the farmer has reaped the main harvest. In other words, I will be grateful for whatever scraps of attention you throw to me. Smile at me once in a while, and I will live upon those smiles."

Phoebe asked, "Do you know the young man who spoke to me a moment ago?"

"Not very well, but I have met him often. He bought the cottage and the pasture that the churlish peasant once owned."

"Don't think that I love him, though I am asking about him. He is only a silly boy, yet he talks well. But what do I care for words? Still, words do well when he who speaks them pleases those who hear them. He is an attractive youth — well, not very attractive. Certainly, he is proud, and yet his pride becomes him. He will make a proper man. The best thing about him is his complexion; and faster than his tongue offended me, his face healed the offense. He is not very tall, yet for his age he is tall. His legs are but so-so, and yet they are good. His lips had a pretty redness — a little riper and more luxurious red than the red of his cheeks. His cheeks' color was just the difference between red and pink.

"Some women, Silvius, had they looked as closely at him as I did, would have almost fallen in love with him. As for me, I neither love him nor hate him. Still, I have more cause to hate him than to love him. What right had he to criticize me the way he did? He said my eyes were black and ugly and my hair was black and ugly. I remember that he scorned me. I am surprised that I didn't criticize him.

"But that does not matter. Omittance is no quittance — just because I didn't criticize him then does not mean that I can't criticize him now. I will write to him a very taunting letter, and you will give it to him. Will you do that, Silvius?"

"Phoebe, with all my heart."

"I will write the letter immediately. The content is in my head and in my heart. I will be bitter with him and very short — exceedingly curt — with him. Let's go, Silvius."

CHAPTER 4

— 4.1 —

In another part of the forest, Rosalind, Celia, and Jaques were talking.

Jaques said to Rosalind, "Please, pretty youth, let me become better acquainted with you."

"They say you are a melancholy fellow."

"I am melancholy. I do love being melancholy better than laughing."

"Those who are either too sad or too merry are abominable fellows and betray themselves to every modern criticism — they are worse than drunkards when it comes to making themselves targets for ridicule."

"Why, it is good to be serious and thoughtful and say nothing."

"Why then, it is good to be a post in the ground. A post says nothing."

"I have my own kind of melancholy. I do not have the scholar's melancholy, which is envious. I do not have the musician's melancholy, which is imaginative. I do not have the courtier's melancholy, which is proud. I do not have the soldier's melancholy, which is ambitious. I do not have the lawyer's melancholy, which is politic. I do not have the lady's melancholy, which is dainty. I do not have the lover's melancholy, which is all of these. I have my own kind of melancholy, which is compounded of many ingredients, extracted from many objects, and indeed the various thoughts inspired by my travels. These thoughts wrap me in a very moody melancholy."

"You are a traveller!" Rosalind said. "By my faith, you have great reason to be melancholic. I am afraid that you may have sold your own lands to see the lands of other men. If that is the case, if you have seen much and have nothing, then you have rich eyes and poor hands."

"Yes, I have gained my experience."

"And your experience makes you sad and serious. I would rather have a fool to make me merry than experience to make me sad, especially if I would have to travel to acquire my sadness!"

Orlando arrived; he was an hour late for his appointment to woo Rosalind.

Orlando said, "Good day and happiness, dear Rosalind!"

Jaques recognized that this sentence was in iambic pentameter. It had five feet of two syllables each with the stress on the second syllable. Unrhymed iambic pentameter is known as blank verse.

Jaques said, "It is time for me to go. May God be with you, if you are going to talk in blank verse."

"Farewell, Monsieur Traveller," Rosalind said. "Since you are a traveller, you ought to act like other travellers. Be sure that you lisp with a cute foreign accent and wear strange suits of foreign fashions. Be sure to disparage all the benefits of your own country, be out of love with the land where you were born, and almost criticize God for making you look like an Englishman. If you don't do these things, I will hardly think you have ridden in a gondola."

Jaques departed.

Rosalind said to Orlando, "How are you, Orlando! Where have you been all this while? You think that you are a lover! If you ever play such another trick on me, do not ever come within my sight."

Orlando objected, "My fair Rosalind, I came within an hour of the time I promised to be here."

"Came within an hour of the time you — who are supposedly a lover — promised to be here! A man who will divide a minute into a thousand parts and break only one part of the thousandth part of a minute in the affairs of love is a man about whom it may be said that Cupid has patted him on the shoulder, but I swear that that man's heart has not been wounded by Cupid's arrow."

"Pardon me, dear Rosalind."

"No. If you are ever again so late for a date, come no more within my sight. I would prefer to be wooed by a snail."

"By a snail?"

"Yes, by a snail," Rosalind said. "Though the snail comes slowly, he carries his house with him. He has something to offer a woman — more than you can offer, I think. Besides, the snail brings its destiny with him."

"What destiny is that?"

"Snails have what look like horns," Rosalind said. "Men who are late for dates must expect to be made cuckolds. The snail comes pre-equipped with horns and therefore knows what to expect."

I get it, Orlando thought. *I had better not be late for dates for Rosalind. If I am late, she will get another boyfriend.*

"Virtuous women are not horn-makers, and my Rosalind is virtuous."

"And I am your Rosalind."

Celia said to Rosalind, "It pleases him to call you Rosalind, but he has a better-looking Rosalind than you."

I get it, Orlando thought. *If I am late for dates, my loved one and her friends will think that I have another girlfriend.*

Rosalind smiled at the expression on Orlando's face, and then she said to him, "Come, woo me, woo me, for now I am in a good mood and likely enough to consent to love you. What would you say to me now, if I were your precious Rosalind?"

"I would kiss her before I spoke."

"No, you had better speak first, and when you were stuck for something to say, then you could kiss her. Very good orators, when they are out of words to say, will spit, but lovers who are out of words to say — God help us! — should take the cleaner option and kiss."

"Suppose Rosalind declines to kiss me?"

"Then you have a new subject to talk about: You can beg her for a kiss."

"Who could be out of words to say when he is with the woman he loves?"

"You had better be out of me than in me if I were your girl — or I would think that my virtue is less impressive than my wit," Rosalind joked.

"Let's talk about a different 'out.' Would I be out of suit?"

"A suit can mean a suit of clothing. If you were in me, you would be out of suit. But given that I am virtuous, you would not be out of your apparel, but you would still be out of your suit — that is, request. I would make you give up your attempt to seduce me. Am I not your Rosalind?"

"I am happy to say that you are, because I want to talk about her."

"Well, let me pretend to be her and say that I will not have you as my boyfriend."

"Then let me be me and say that I will die."

"Do not yourself die. Die by proxy — have a lawyer act for you by proxy. But seriously, people have examined the verses of the Bible and concluded that this poor world is almost six thousand years old, and in all that time not one man has died in real life because of love. Troilus loved Cressida, but he had his brains dashed out with a Greek club, yet he did what he could to die from love before he died from the club and he is regarded as an exemplary lover.

Leander would have lived for many happy years, even if his loved one, Hero, had become a nun, if it had not been for a hot midsummer night. Leander, that good youth, went into the Hellespont to wash himself but started cramping and was drowned. The foolish coroners of that age said that the cause of his death was his love for Hero of Sestos. They said that he drowned when a storm arose while he was swimming in the Hellespont to visit his lover. All of these tales of men who have died from love are lies. Men have died from time to time and worms have eaten them, but the men did not die because of love."

"I do not want the real Rosalind to think like this. I believe that her frown might kill me."

"Trust me, her frown will not kill a fly."

I get it, Orlando thought. *Some of the ideas of romantic love are exaggerated. Still, love really does exist.*

Rosalind said, "But come, now I will be your Rosalind in a more agreeable mood. Ask me for whatever you want. I will grant it."

"Then love me, Rosalind."

"Yes, I will — on Fridays and Saturdays and all the other days of the week."

"And so you will have me?"

"Yes, and twenty more men like you."

"What are you saying?"

"Aren't you good?"

"I hope so."

"Can one desire too much of a good thing?"

I get it, Orlando thought. *Rosalind has a healthy interest in having sex, and it is a good idea for me to marry her so that each of us is committed to the other.*

Rosalind said to Celia, who had been listening to and laughing at the conversation between Rosalind and Orlando, "Come, sister, you shall be the priest and marry us."

She added, "Give me your hand, Orlando. What do you say, sister?"

Orlando said, "Please, marry us."

Celia was laughing hard. She said, "I cannot say the words."

Rosalind pretended that Celia had forgotten words that no woman who was either married or wanted to be married would forget: "You must begin, 'Will you, Orlando — '"

"OK," Celia said, "Will you, Orlando, take Rosalind to be your lawfully wedded wife?"

"I will."

Rosalind knew that "will" is not the same as "do." She wanted a real commitment, and so she asked, "Yes, but when?"

"Right now, as fast as Aliena can marry us."

"Then you must say, 'I take you, Rosalind, as my lawfully wedded wife.'"

"I take you, Rosalind, as my lawfully wedded wife."

I get it, Orlando thought. *Rosalind wants a real commitment, not a promise to be committed.*

Rosalind said to Celia, "I should ask you for the wedding license. But I do take you, Orlando, as my lawfully wedded husband."

I get it, Orlando thought. *If I make a commitment to Rosalind, she will make a commitment to me.*

Rosalind added, "I am a girl who has raced ahead of the priest and answered the priest's question before he even asked it — a woman's thought always runs ahead of her actions."

"All thoughts are like that — they are winged."

"Now tell me how long you would have her after you have possessed her — that is, married her and slept with her."

"Forever and a day."

"Say 'for a day.' Leave out the 'forever.' No, no, Orlando. Men are April when they woo, and December when they wed. Virgins are May when they are virgins, but the sky changes when they are wives. I will be more jealous of you than a Barbary cock-pigeon is of his hen, more clamorous than a parrot protesting against rain, more fond of novelty than an ape, more changeable in my desires than a monkey. I will weep for nothing, like a statue of Diana gushing water in a fountain — I will do that when you are disposed to be merry. I will laugh like a hyena when you want to go to sleep."

"Will my Rosalind act like that?"

"I swear by my life that she will act the way that I act."

I get it, Orlando thought. *The first flush of romantic love will not last. At times Rosalind will get on my nerves, and no doubt at times I will get on her nerves. But even though the first flush of romantic love will not last, a committed relationship can last.*

"But Rosalind is wise."

"Or else she would not have the wit to act like this. The wiser she is, the more wayward she will be. Close the doors upon a woman's wit, and it will fly out of the window. Shut the window, and it will fly out of the keyhole. Stop up the keyhole, and it will fly out the chimney with the smoke."

"A man who had a wife with such a wit, he might say to her, 'Wit, where do you wander? What are you thinking! Where are your senses!'"

"You may want to wait to say that when you see your wife's wit going to your neighbor's bed."

"And what wit could have wit enough to make an excuse for that?"

"She would say that she went to seek you there. You shall never find her without her excuse, unless you find her without a tongue. Any woman who cannot make her sin the fault of her husband should never breastfeed her child — because her child will turn out to be a fool. Breast-fed children get either wisdom or foolishness from the milk of the mother."

I get it, Orlando thought. *A good marriage will consist of years of happiness. A bad marriage will consist of years of unhappiness. An unhappy wife can make her husband's life a living Hell. A happy wife can make her husband's life a living Heaven. A wise husband will not ignore his wife. He will pay attention to her, and he will show up when he tells her he will show up — or have a damn good reason for not showing up. Before and after I marry Rosalind, I had better treat her right. And if I treat her right, I am sure that she will treat me right.*

He said, "For the next two hours, Rosalind, I will have to leave you."

Rosalind assumed an overly dramatic, joking tone: "No, dear love! I cannot be away from you for two whole hours!"

"I must have dinner with Duke Senior. By two o'clock I will be with you again."

Rosalind continued with an overly dramatic, joking tone: "Yes, go on your way. Go on your way. I knew the kind of man whom you would turn out to be: a faithless lover. My friends told me as much, and I thought no less. Your flattering tongue won me over. But don't worry about it. I am just one more woman who has been cast away and so I will die!"

Both Rosalind and Orlando smiled. No man had ever died of love — and neither had any woman.

Rosalind asked, seriously, "So you will return at two o'clock?"

"Yes, sweet Rosalind."

I mean it, Orlando thought, *I have learned my lesson. If I don't come on time, I will have a damn good reason.*

Rosalind said, "I swear, and I mean it — so help me, God — and I also swear the pretty little oaths that lovers swear that if you break even the tiniest part of your promise or come even one minute late, I will think you the most pathetic breaker of promises and the most hollow lover and the most unworthy of her whom you call Rosalind who may be chosen out of the gross band of the unfaithful lovers. Therefore, beware my anger and keep your promise."

"I will keep my promise as religiously as I would if you were really Rosalind. Goodbye."

"Well, Time is the old judge who examines all such offenders, and so Time will determine the truth of your promise. When the time comes for you to return here, we will see if you are actually here. Goodbye."

Orlando departed.

Celia, who had been amused by the conversation between Rosalind and Orlando, said to Rosalind, "You have severely criticized all women in your love-talk with Orlando. We women should remove all your male clothing and show the world first that you are a female and second that like a foul bird, you have dirtied your own nest."

"Oh, cousin, cousin, cousin, my pretty cousin, I wish that you knew how many fathoms deep I am in love! But the depth of my love cannot be sounded: My affection has an unknown bottom, like the bay of Portugal. My love is so deep that it cannot be measured."

"Or, rather, your love is bottomless. As fast as you pour in love, it runs out."

"No, let Cupid judge how deeply in love I am. Let Cupid, that same wicked bastard of Venus, who conceived during an affair with Mercury, who was not her husband, judge how deeply in love I am. Let that same wicked bastard, who was the result of an impulse and was born of madness, judge how deeply in love I am. Let Cupid, that blind rascally boy who abuses everyone's eyes because his own are out, judge how deeply in love I am. Cupid is blindfolded when he shoots his arrows, and they cause people to look at each other differently. I tell you, Aliena, that I cannot stand being away from Orlando: I will go and find a shadowy place and sigh until he returns."

Aliena replied, "And I will take a nap."

— 4.2 —

Jaques and some Lords, who were dressed like foresters, had been hunting in the forest. The hunt had been successful; they had killed a horned stag.

Jaques asked, "Whose shot killed the deer?"

One of the Lords replied, "Sir, it was my shot."

"Let us present this Lord to Duke Senior in a triumphal procession as if he were a Roman conqueror," Jaques said. "We should set the stag's horns on this Lord's head to serve as a victorious wreath."

He asked a forester, "Do you have a song that is right for this occasion?"

"Yes, sir."

"Sing it. It does not matter whether it is in tune, as long as it makes enough noise."

The forester sang, "*What shall he have who killed the deer?*

"*He shall have the deer's leather skin and horns to wear.*

"*Then let us sing to him as we go home.*"

The other Lords picked up the carcass of the deer and started to carry it back to their camp.

The forester sang, "*Do not scorn to wear the horn;*

"*It was a crest before you were born:*

"*Your father's father wore it,*

"*And your father bore it:*

"*The horn, the horn, the lusty horn*

"*Is not a thing to laugh at and to scorn.*"

— 4.3 —

Rosalind and Celia were talking.

Rosalind said, "What do you say now? Isn't it past two o'clock? Orlando is not here!"

Celia said, "I promise you that with pure love and troubled brain, he has taken his bow and arrows, told everyone that he was going hunting, and set off to take a nap. Most lovers can't sleep because they are thinking about their beloved. Orlando is not like that."

She added, "Look at who is coming now."

Silvius, carrying a letter, walked up to them and said to Rosalind, "My errand is to you, fair youth. My gentle Phoebe asked me to give you this letter. I do not know its contents, but judging by Phoebe's stern expression and angry and waspish movements while she was writing it, it must bear an angry message. Please pardon me. I am only a guiltless messenger."

Rosalind read the letter and said, "Patience herself would be shocked by this letter and want to start a fight. If I can bear this letter, then I can bear anything. Phoebe writes that I am not handsome and that I lack manners. She calls me proud, and she says that she could not love me even if men were rare as the phoenix. Since only one phoenix lives at a time, reproducing by cremating its old self and arising anew from the ashes, Phoenix is telling me that she would not love me if I were the last man on Earth. My God! But why is she writing to me? I do not want her love — her love is not the hare that I am hunting."

She said to Silvius, "Shepherd, you wrote this."

"No, I did not," Silvius protested. "I did not know its contents. Phoebe wrote it."

"No, you are a fool if you think that I will believe that. You wrote this letter because you love Phoebe — you are now the most foolish kind of lover. I saw her hands. She has hands like leather. Her hands are brown like the color of sandstone. Truly, I thought that she was wearing gloves, but those were really her hands. She has the hands of a hard-working housewife, but that does not matter. I say that she did not write this letter. This letter was written by a man in a man's handwriting."

"No, this is her letter and her handwriting."

"Why, this letter is written in a boisterous and cruel style — a style fit for someone who is looking for a fight. Why, she challenges me to fight like a Muslim Turk challenges a Christian to fight. The gentle brain of a woman could not write such outrageously rude sentences and such black words — they are blacker in meaning than the ink in which they are written on the page. Would you like to hear me read this letter out loud?"

"Yes, please, because I do not know what Phoebe says in the letter, although I have heard too many of Phoebe's cruel words."

"Phoebe has Phoebe-ed you in the past. Now she is Phoebe-ing me. Listen to the words that the tyrant wrote."

Rosalind read out loud, "*Are you a god into a shepherd turned,*

"*So that a maiden's heart you can have burned?*"

Rosalind commented, "Can a woman rant and rave like this?"

Silvius said, "Do you call that ranting and raving!"

Rosalind read out loud, "*Why, having laid your godhead apart,*

"*Are you warring with a woman's heart?*"

Rosalind commented, "Did you ever hear such ranting and raving?"

Rosalind read out loud, "*Whiles the eyes of man did woo me,*

"*They could do no harm to me.*"

Rosalind commented, "Men could not hurt her. In other words, she is calling me a beast."

Rosalind read out loud, "*If the scorn of your bright eyes*

"*Has power to raise such love in my eyes,*

"*Then in me what strange effect*

"*Would they work if you looked at me with kind aspect!*

"*While you criticized me, you I did love;*

"*How then might your prayers move!*

"*He who brings this love letter to thee*

"*Little knows this love in me:*

"*And by him send a sealed letter that tells me your mind;*

"*Whether that your youth and disposition kind*

"*Will the faithful offer take*

"*Of me and all that I can make;*

"*Or else by him my love deny,*

"*And then I'll think about how I will die.*"

Silvius said, "This is a love letter to you! She is not at all challenging you to a fight!"

"Poor shepherd!" Celia said to Silvius.

"Do you pity Silvius?" Rosalind asked Celia. "Don't! He deserves no pity."

Rosalind said to Silvius, "Will you love such a woman as Phoebe? Why? She has used you! She has made you an instrument and is playing bad music on you! She has used you to carry her love letter to another man! Well, go back to her, for I can see that love has made you a tame snake — your snake is tame. Tell her that if she loves me, I order her to love you. If she will not love you, I will never have her unless you beg me to have her. If you are a true lover, leave immediately and don't say a word."

She looked up and said to Celia, "Here comes more company."

Silvius departed, and Oliver, the oldest brother of Orlando, walked up to Rosalind and Celia, who of course did not recognize him.

"Good day, pretty women," Oliver said courteously. "Please tell me, if you know, where in this part of the forest stands a shepherd's cottage in a grove of olive trees?"

Celia replied, "It is west of here, in a neighboring valley. The row of willows by the murmuring stream will take you to the cottage if you keep the willows on your right side. But at this time of day, the cottage stands empty. No one is at home."

Oliver replied, "If my eye has profited from my hearing, then I know who you are from the description I have heard of you: 'The boy is good looking, feminine, and carries himself as if he were an older sister. The woman is short and darker than her brother.' Are you the owners of the cottage I asked about?"

"It is no boast, since you have asked us directly, to say that we are the owners of that cottage," Celia replied.

"Orlando sends his regards to both of you, and to that youth whom he calls his Rosalind, he sends this bloody handkerchief," Oliver said.

Then he asked Rosalind, "Are you that youth?"

"I am, but what does all of this mean?"

"I will have to tell you some shameful things about myself if you want to know who I am — and how, and why, and where Orlando's handkerchief was stained with blood."

"Please, tell us your story," Celia said.

"When Orlando recently departed from you, he made a promise to return again in an hour."

Rosalind thought, *Actually, within two hours. Apparently, Orlando wanted to make sure that he got here on time.*

Oliver continued, "But while he was walking in this forest, thinking both bitter and sweet thoughts of love, something happened. He glanced to the side, and saw something unexpected. Under an oak, whose boughs were mossy with age and whose aged top was bare and dry, he saw a wretched ragged man with long, wild hair lying on his back and sleeping. A green and gold snake had wreathed itself around this man's neck and its threatening head was approaching his open mouth. Suddenly, seeing Orlando, it unwrapped itself from the man's neck and zigzagged away and slithered under a bush in whose shade a lioness, with udders all sucked dry by its cubs, lay crouching with its head on the ground. With catlike patience, it watched to see when the sleeping man should get up because lions and lionesses — the monarchs of the animal kingdom — will not prey on anything that seems to be dead. Seeing this, Orlando approached the man and discovered that the man was his oldest brother."

"I have heard him speak of that same brother," Celia said. "He called him the most unnatural brother and the most lacking in brotherly love who ever lived among men."

"And well might Orlando describe him in that way because I know for myself that his oldest brother was exactly like that."

"What did Orlando do?" Rosalind asked. "Did he leave him there to be food for the suckled and hungry lioness?"

"Twice he turned his back on his oldest brother and thought to leave him there, but his natural affection was stronger even than his desire for revenge, and his nature was stronger than his desire to give his oldest brother the just desserts that he had earned. Therefore, Orlando battled and quickly defeated the lioness. Hearing the noise of that battle, I awoke."

"Are you Orlando's oldest brother?" Celia asked.

"Was it you whom he rescued?" Rosalind asked.

"Was it you who so often plotted to kill him?" Celia asked.

"It was I, but it is not I," Oliver replied. "I do not stop myself from telling you what kind of man I was, since my conversion to a better kind of man tastes so sweet."

"But what about the bloody handkerchief?" Rosalind asked.

"I'm coming to that. When my brother and I had tearfully told our stories from the first part to the last part, and I had, for example, told him how I came to be in that deserted part of the forest, Orlando led me to Duke Senior, who gave me fresh clothing and a meal and then placed me in Orlando's care. Orlando then led me to his cave. There he stripped off his clothing, and I saw that the lioness had torn some of the flesh of his arm away. All this time, Orlando had bled, and now he fainted, and as he fainted, he cried out the name of Rosalind. To tell the rest of the story briefly, I revived him and bound up his wound. After a short time, Orlando — being strong at heart — sent me here, stranger as I am, to tell you this story so that you might excuse his broken promise. He wanted me to give this napkin dyed in his blood to the shepherd youth he calls Rosalind."

Hearing that it was Orlando's blood on the handkerchief, Rosalind fainted.

"Ganymede! Sweet Ganymede!" Celia cried.

"Many people faint when they see blood," Oliver said.

"In this case, there is more to it," Celia said. "Cousin Ganymede!"

Celia was so upset that she did not call Ganymede "Brother Ganymede."

"Look, he is regaining consciousness," Oliver said.

"I wish I were at home," Rosalind said.

"We'll lead you there," Celia said.

She said to Oliver, "Please, take him by the arm."

"Be of good cheer, young man," Oliver said. "But are you a man? You lack the heart of a man."

"I do lack the heart of a man — I confess it," Rosalind said.

She paused, recovered somewhat, and then added, "Anyone would think my faint was well counterfeited! I put on a good act! Please, tell your brother how well I pretended to faint. Heigh-ho!"

"This was no counterfeit," Oliver said. "You did not fake your faint. Your face is too pale for me to believe that you faked this. You genuinely fainted."

"I faked it, I assure you," Rosalind said. "I am a good actor."

"Well, then, be brave and fake being a man," Oliver said.

"So I do," Rosalind said, "but, truly and rightfully, I should have been a woman."

"Come, Ganymede, you look paler and paler. Please, let's go home."

Celia said to Orlando, "Good sir, come with us."

"Yes, I will," Oliver said. "I must bear back to Orlando the news of whether or not you will excuse him for his absence, Rosalind."

"I will think about my answer," Rosalind said, "but tell him how well I faked my faint. Let's go."

Oliver and Celia held on to Rosalind's arms and helped her walk to the cottage.

CHAPTER 5

— 5.1 —

Touchstone and Audrey were talking about getting married.

"We shall find a time to be married, Audrey. Be patient, gentle Audrey."

"The priest — Sir Oliver Martext — was good enough to marry us, despite everything that the old gentleman — Jaques — said."

"He was a most wicked Sir Oliver, Audrey. He was a most vile Martext. But, Audrey, I have heard that a young man here in the forest lays claim to you — like me, he wants to marry you."

"Yes, I know who he is. His name is William, but he has no legal claim on me. I have already said that I want to marry you. Look. Here comes the man you mean."

"It is meat and drink to me to see a hick. Indeed, we who have good wits have much to answer for. We are always making fun of hicks. We cannot restrain ourselves."

William politely said, "Good day, Audrey."

"Good day to you, William."

William politely said to Touchstone, "And good day to you, sir."

"Good day, gentle friend. Cover your head — you don't need to take off your hat to show me respect. Please cover your head. How old are you, friend?"

"Twenty-five, sir."

"A mature age. Is your name William?"

"Yes, sir."

"It is a good name. Were you born in the forest here?"

"Yes, sir, thank God."

"'Thank God.' That is a good thing to say. Are you rich?"

"Moderately, sir."

"'Moderately' is a good answer, a very excellent answer, but wait, it is not. It is a moderately good answer. Are you wise?"

"Yes, sir, I have a good mind."

"Why, you say well, but I do now remember a saying: 'The fool thinks that he is wise, but the wise man knows that he is a fool.' The heathen philosopher, when he had a desire to eat a grape, would open his lips when he put it into his mouth. This taught other people that grapes were made to eat and lips to open. Do you love Audrey?"

"Yes, I do, sir."

"Give me your hand. Are you learned? Are you educated?"

"No, sir."

"Then learn this from me: To have is to have. It is a figure of speech in rhetoric that drink, being poured out of a cup into a glass, by filling the one empties the other; for all well-known writers do agree that the Latin word '*ipse*' means he. Now know this: You are not *ipse*, for I am he."

"Which he, sir?"

"The he, sir, who will marry Audrey. Therefore, you hick, abandon — which in the vulgar language means leave — the society — which boorish people call company — of this female — which in the common language is woman. Put all this together, and it means this: Either you abandon the society of this female, or you will perish, hick. Or, to say it in words that you will understand, you will die. To make it absolutely clear, I will kill you, make you go to a better world, translate your life into death, translate your liberty into bondage. I will poison you, or beat you with a club, or put a steel sword in you. I will fight you in a duel. I will overwhelm you with crafty plots. I will kill you in a hundred and fifty different ways, so therefore tremble and depart."

"Do go away, good William," Audrey said.

William looked at Audrey. It was clear that she preferred to marry Touchstone, so William said politely to Touchstone, "God bless you, sir," and then he walked away.

Corin now arrived on the scene and said to Touchstone, "Ganymede and Aliena are looking for you. Come quickly!"

"Let's hurry, Audrey," Touchstone said.

He said to Corin, "I'm coming. I'm coming."

— 5.2 —

In another part of the forest, Orlando said to Oliver, "Is it possible that on so little acquaintance you should have fallen in love with Aliena? That as soon as you saw her, you loved her? That as soon as you loved her, you wooed her? That, as soon as you wooed her, she agreed to marry you? Do you really mean to marry her?"

Oliver replied, "Do not criticize the giddiness — the haste — of these events. Do not criticize her poverty, the short time she and I have known each other, my sudden wooing of her, or her quick agreement to marry me. Instead, be like me and love Aliena. Say with me, 'I love Aliena.' Say with her that she loves me. Give your consent to this marriage so that she and I may live happily married together. This will work out to your advantage. I will give to you our father's house and his estate that he bequeathed to me. I will live here and die here as a shepherd."

"You have my consent to marry Aliena," Orlando said. "Let your wedding be tomorrow. I will invite Duke Senior and all of his happy followers to the wedding. Go to Aliena and prepare for the wedding."

Orlando added, "Look, here comes my Rosalind."

Rosalind walked up to them and said to Oliver, "God bless you, brother-in-law," meaning that they would become in-laws because Oliver would marry Aliena, Ganymede's "sister."

"God bless you, fair sister-in-law," Oliver said. Like Orlando, he referred to Rosalind as a female, ignoring her disguise as Ganymede.

Oliver departed.

Rosalind said, "My dear Orlando, how it grieves me to see you wear your heart in a sling!"

"It is my arm."

"I thought that your heart had been wounded with the claws of a lion."

"My heart has been wounded, but by the eyes of a lady."

"Did your brother tell you how I counterfeited a faint when he showed me your handkerchief?"

"Yes, he did, and he told me greater wonders than that."

Rosalind thought, *He told you of his sudden love for Celia. I wonder if he told you of any other wonders.*

She said, "I know what you mean: the upcoming marriage. It is true that nothing was ever so sudden except the fight of two rams charging at each other and trying to hurt each other, and Julius Caesar's theatrical brag of 'I came, saw, and overcame.' Your brother and my sister no sooner met but they looked at each other, no sooner looked at each other but they loved each other, no sooner loved each other but they sighed, no sooner sighed but they asked one another the reason for the sigh, no sooner knew the reason for the sigh but they sought a remedy to stop the sighs.

"In doing these things, they have made a pair of stairs leading to marriage. They will have to climb those stairs quickly, or they will enjoy the honeymoon before they enjoy the wedding ceremony. They are in the very passion of love and they must be together — clubs cannot part them."

"They shall be married tomorrow, and I will invite the Duke to the wedding," Orlando said. "But how bitter it is to look at happiness through another man's eyes! Tomorrow my heart will be heavier than ever because I have not gotten what I wish for and must look at how happy my brother is because he has gotten what he wished for."

"Do you want me to pretend to be Rosalind for you tomorrow?"

"I can live no longer by merely imagining what I want instead of actually having it."

Rosalind thought, *Orlando has matured. He is ready to marry.*

"I will weary you then no longer with idle talk," Rosalind said. "Listen to me. I will tell you something important. I know that you are a gentleman of good intelligence. I am not telling you this so that you should think that I am smart because I think that you are smart. I also am not trying to acquire a greater reputation except that I am trying to get you to believe that I want to help you. Believe, please, that I can do strange things. I have, since I was three years old, studied with a magician who is most knowledgeable in his white art and who does not practice damnable black magic.

"If you really love Rosalind as much as your behavior says you do, then when your brother marries Aliena, you shall marry Rosalind. I know into what circumstances of fortune she is driven; and it is not impossible to me, if it appears not inappropriate to you, to set her before your eyes tomorrow. She will be her own human self and not a phantom. Your soul shall not be in danger."

"Do you really mean that you can do these things?"

"Yes, I do. I swear it by my life, which I value highly. I am a magician, but I am a white magician. Therefore, put your best clothes on and invite your friends to your wedding. If you want to be married tomorrow, you will be. And if you want to marry Rosalind tomorrow, you will."

Rosalind heard a noise. She looked around, saw Phoebe and Silvius, and said, "Look, here comes a lover of mine and a lover of hers."

Phoebe, who was angry, said to Rosalind, "Young man, you have done me much discourtesy. You showed Silvius the letter that I wrote to you."

"I do not care," Rosalind said. "It is my deliberate intention to be despiteful and discourteous to you. You are being followed by a faithful shepherd — Silvius — look at him and love him because he worships you."

Phoebe said, "Good shepherd, tell this youth what it is to love."

"It is to do nothing but sigh and weep, and so do I for Phoebe."

Phoebe said, "And I for Ganymede."

Orlando said, "And I for Rosalind."

Rosalind said, "And I for no woman."

Silvius added, "It is to be entirely faithful and full of devotion for the loved one, and so am I for Phoebe."

Phoebe said, "And I for Ganymede."

Orlando said, "And I for Rosalind."

Rosalind said, "And I for no woman."

Silvius added, "It is to live in a world of the imagination, a dream world, with emotions and wishes, with adoration, duty, and obedience, with humbleness, patience and impatience, purity, endurance, and dutiful respect, and so live I for Phoebe."

Phoebe said, "And I for Ganymede."

Orlando said, "And I for Rosalind."

Rosalind said, "And I for no woman."

Phoebe said to Rosalind, "If this is true, why do you blame me for loving you?"

Silvius said to Phoebe, "If this is true, why do you blame me for loving you?"

Orlando said, "If this is true, why do you blame me for loving you?"

Rosalind asked Orlando, "To whom are you speaking?"

"To Rosalind — a woman who is not here, and who does not hear me."

"Please, no more of this," Rosalind said. "It is like the howling of Irish wolves at the Moon."

Rosalind said to Silvius, "I will help you, if I can."

She said to Phoebe, "I would love you, if I could."

She said to everyone, "Tomorrow, all of you meet me as a group."

She said to Phoebe, "I will marry you, if I ever marry a woman, and I will be married tomorrow."

She said to Orlando, "I will satisfy you, if ever I satisfied a man, and you will be married tomorrow."

She said to Silvius, "I will content you, if what pleases you will content you, and you will be married tomorrow."

She said to Orlando, "As you love Rosalind, meet me tomorrow."

She said to Silvius, "As you love Phoebe, meet me tomorrow."

She added, "And as I love no woman, I will meet all of you tomorrow. So farewell. Remember the commands that I have given to you."

"I will not fail to meet you tomorrow, if I am alive," Silvius said.

"Nor I," Phoebe said.

"Nor I," Orlando said.

— 5.3 —

In another part of the forest, Touchstone said, "Tomorrow is the joyful day, Audrey. Tomorrow we will be married."

"I want to marry you with all my heart," Audrey said, "and I hope it is not an unchaste desire to really want to be a married woman."

She looked up and said, "Look, here come two of the banished Duke's pages."

One of the pages said to Touchstone, "Hello, honorable gentleman."

"Hello," Touchstone replied. "Come, sit down, and sing a song."

"We will sing," the other page said. He joked, "Sit in the middle," referring to a song with a lyric about "the fool in the middle."

The first page asked, "Shall we begin singing at once, without hawking or spitting or saying we are hoarse, which are the prologues before the singing of a bad voice?"

"Yes, let us begin singing immediately," the other page said, "and let us both sing in unison. We shall sing like two gypsies riding on one horse."

They sang this song:

"*It was a lover and his lass,*
"*With a hey, and a ho, and a hey nonino,*
"*That over the green wheat field did pass*
"*In the springtime, the only pretty marriage- and ring-time,*
"*When birds do sing, hey ding a ding, ding:*
"*Sweet lovers love the spring.*
"*Between the rows of the rye,*
"*With a hey, and a ho, and a hey nonino*
"*These pretty country folks would lie,*
"*In the springtime, the only pretty marriage- and ring-time,*
"*When birds do sing, hey ding a ding, ding:*
"*Sweet lovers love the spring.*
"*This carol they began that hour,*
"*With a hey, and a ho, and a hey nonino,*
"*How that a life was as brief as the life of a flower*
"*In the springtime, the only pretty marriage- and ring-time,*

"*When birds do sing, hey ding a ding, ding:*
"*Sweet lovers love the spring.*
"*And therefore seize the present time,*
"*With a hey, and a ho, and a hey nonino;*
"*For love is crowned with the spring — the prime —*
"*In the springtime, the only pretty marriage- and ring-time,*
"*When birds do sing, hey ding a ding, ding:*
"*Sweet lovers love the spring.*"

Touchstone said, "Truly, young gentlemen, though there was no great content in the ditty, yet the song was sung out of tune."

"You are deceived, sir," a page said. "We kept time, we lost not our time. We kept the rhythm."

"You did lose the time," Touchstone replied. "I consider it but time lost to hear such a foolish song. May God be with you, and may God mend your voices! Come, Audrey. Let's go."

Touchstone thought, *The song had content.* Carpe diem. *Seize the day. Gather ye rosebuds while ye may. What are the young lovers doing between the rows of the rye? The he is giving the she a green gown. Their activity results in the girl getting grass stains on the back of her gown. I was overly critical. Why? People expect me to be overly critical. Being overly critical is a way to be funny and make puns about time.*

— 5.4 —

Duke Senior, Amiens, Jaques, Orlando, Oliver, and Celia were gathered together.

Duke Senor asked, "Do you believe, Orlando, that the young Ganymede can do everything that he has promised?"

"I sometimes do believe that he can, and sometimes I do not. I am like those people who are afraid that their hopes are unfounded and are afraid that they will be disappointed."

Rosalind, Silvius, and Phoebe now arrived.

Rosalind said, "Everybody, be patient once more, while we review our agreement."

Rosalind said to Duke Senior, "You say that if I bring here your Rosalind, you will give her away in marriage to Orlando here?"

"Yes, I will, and I would even if I had kingdoms to give away with her."

Rosalind said to Orlando, "And you say that you will marry her, if I bring her here?"

"Yes, I will, and I would even if I were of all kingdoms King."

Rosalind said to Phoebe, "You say that you will marry me, if I am willing to marry you?"

"Yes, I will, and I would even if I were to die one hour later."

Rosalind said to Phoebe, "But if you refuse to marry me, you say that you will marry this most faithful shepherd, whose name is Silvius?"

"That is the agreement we have made."

Rosalind said to Silvius, "You say that you will marry Phoebe, if she is willing to marry you?"

"Yes, I will, and I would even if marriage to her and death were the same thing."

Rosalind said, "And I have said that I will straighten everything out."

She then talked to several people in order:

"Keep your word, Duke Senior, to give away your daughter in marriage.

"Keep your word, Orlando, to marry Duke Senior's daughter.

"Keep your word, Phoebe, that you will marry me, or if you refuse to marry me, that you will marry instead this shepherd, Silvius.

"Keep your word, Silvius, that you will marry Phoebe if she refuses to marry me.

"Now I will leave to make all these things come true."

Rosalind and Celia left the others.

Duke Senior said, "I do see in this shepherd boy, Ganymede, some things that remind me of my daughter's appearance."

Orlando said, "My Lord, the first time that I ever saw him, I thought that he was a brother to your daughter. But, my good Lord, this boy was born in the forest, and he has been tutored in the fundamentals of many dangerous and magical studies by his uncle, who he says is a great magician, hidden in the circle of this forest."

Touchstone and Audrey arrived.

Jaques said, "Apparently, another great Biblical flood is coming, and these couples are coming to the ark. Here comes a pair of very strange beasts, which in all tongues are called fools."

"Salutation and greeting to you all!" Touchstone said.

"My good Lord, bid him welcome," Jaques said to Duke Senior. "This is the motley-minded gentleman that I have so often met in the forest. He swears that he has been a courtier."

Touchstone said, "If any man doubts that, let him put me to the test. I have trod a slow, stately dance. I have flattered a lady; I have been hypocritical with my friend and deceptively courteous with my enemy. I have ruined three tailors by not paying my bills. I have had four quarrels, and I almost fought one duel."

"How was the duel settled?" Jaques asked.

"I met with the man with whom I had quarreled, and we discovered that the quarrel rested upon the seventh cause," Touchstone said.

"What is the seventh cause?" Jaques asked.

Jaques then added, "My good Lord, I hope that you like this fellow."

Duke Senior replied, "I like him very well."

"Thank you, sir. I return the compliment," Touchstone said to Duke Senior. "I have pressed in here, sir, amongst the rest of the country copulatives who wish to be married, to swear to be faithful and to forswear to be unfaithful. Marriage requires us to be faithful, but blood — sexual passion — sometimes makes us want to break our vow to be faithful. This woman is a poor virgin, an ugly thing, but my own. It is a whim of mine, sir, to take that which no other man will. Rich chastity dwells like a miser, sir, in a poor house — it is like a beautiful pearl in a foul oyster."

Duke Senior said to Jaques about Touchstone, "Truly, he is very quick and full of sense and intelligence."

Touchstone said, "According to the fool's bolt, sir, and such dulcet diseases. Remember: A fool's bolt — that is, his arrow or wit — is soon shot. Like other fools, I quickly let my arrows fly. For fools, that is a sweet disease."

Jaques asked, "What about the seventh cause? What did you mean by saying that the quarrel rested upon the seventh cause?"

Touchstone said, "The quarrel rested upon a lie seven times removed."

He said to Audrey, "Keep your knees together, Audrey."

Then he said, "Let me explain, sir. I disliked the cut of a certain courtier's beard. He sent me word that if I said his beard was not cut well, he was of the opinion that it was cut well. This is called the Retort Courteous.

"If I sent him word again that it was not well cut, he would send me word that he cut it to please himself. This is called the Quip Modest.

"If I sent him word again that it was not well cut, he would send me word that he did not value my judgment. This is called the Reply Churlish.

"If I sent him word again that it was not well cut, he would answer that I did not speak the truth. This is called the Reproof Valiant.

"If I sent him word again that it was not well cut, he would say that I lied. This is called the Counter-cheque Quarrelsome.

"The two that are left are the Lie Circumstantial and the Lie Direct."

"How often did you say that his beard was not well cut?" Jaques asked.

"I dared go no further than the Lie Circumstantial, and he dared not give me the Lie Direct, and so we measured swords, said that they were uneven in length and therefore fighting a duel would not be fair combat, and we parted."

"Can you name again the degrees of the lie?" Jaques asked.

"Of course, sir. We have books that tell us how to quarrel with each other without breaking any rules. They are like books of etiquette for quarreling. I will name you the degrees of the lie: The first, the Retort Courteous; the second, the Quip Modest; the third, the Reply Churlish; the fourth, the Reproof Valiant; the fifth, the Counter-cheque Quarrelsome; the sixth, the Lie with Circumstance; the seventh, the Lie Direct. All of these you may say but avoid fighting a duel except for the Lie Direct, and even with that you may avoid fighting a duel if you use an If. I knew of one case when seven justices could not settle a quarrel, but when the two arguing parties met together, one of them thought of an If: 'If you said this, then I said that.' The two parties shook hands and swore to be brothers. The word 'If' is a remarkable peacemaker; there is much virtue in the word 'If.'"

Jaques said to Duke Senior, "Isn't this jester a rare fellow, my Lord? He's as good as this when speaking on any subject, and yet he is a fool."

"He uses his reputation as a fool to sneak up on people and shoot his arrows of wit at them," Duke Senior said.

Low, soft music played. Rosalind and Celia now appeared. They were wearing women's clothing, and they had brought Hymen, the male god of marriage ceremonies, with them.

Hymen said, "There is laughter in heaven when earthly affairs are put right and people are as one."

Hymen said to Duke Senior, "Good Duke, greet your daughter, Rosalind. I, Hymen from Heaven, brought her to you. Yes, I brought her here so that you could join Rosalind's hand with Orlando's hand. They have pledged their hearts to each other."

Rosalind said to her father, Duke Senior, "To you I give myself, for I am yours."

Rosalind said to her beloved, Orlando, "To you I give myself, for I am yours."

Duke Senior said to Rosalind, "If there is truth in sight, you are my daughter."

Orlando said to Rosalind, "If there is truth in sight, you are my Rosalind."

A disappointed Phoebe said, "If sight and shape are true, why then, my love adieu!"

Rosalind said to Duke Senior, "I will have no father, if you are not he."

Rosalind said to Orlando, "I will have no husband, if you are not he."

Rosalind said to Phoebe, "I will never wed a woman, if you are not she."

"Quiet!" Hymen ordered. "I will banish confusion by making all these strange events clear. Here are eight people who must take hands and be married, if truth is true."

Hymen said to Orlando and Rosalind, "You and you no cross shall part. No argument shall ever separate you."

Hymen said to Oliver and Celia, "You and you are heart in heart. You have given your hearts to each other."

Hymen said to Phoebe, "You to his love must accord, or have a woman as your Lord. Unless you marry Silvius, Rosalind will be your husband."

Hymen said to Touchstone and Audrey, "You and you are securely bound together, like winter and foul weather."

Hymen said to the four couples, "While we sing a wedding hymn, all of you will talk to each other and ask each other questions. Satisfy your curiosity. Discuss how you came here, and talk about your upcoming marriages. That way, your amazement will diminish."

Many people sang this song:

"*Wedding is the crown that great Juno, goddess of marriage, wears,*

"*O blessed bond of board and bed!*

"*It is Hymen — marriage — who peoples every town.*

"*Solemn wedlock then be honored.*

"*Honor, solemn honor and renown,*

"*Is due to Hymen, the god of every town!*"

Duke Senior said to Celia, "My dear niece, you are as welcome here as is my daughter."

Phoebe said to Silvius, "I will not go back on my promise. You will be my husband. Your faithfulness to me makes me love you. We are one."

Jaques de Boys, the brother of Oliver and Orlando, suddenly arrived with news.

He said, "Let me say a few words. I am the second son of old Sir Rowland, and I bring these tidings to this fair assembly. Duke Frederick, hearing that every day men of high rank resorted to this forest, made ready a mighty army. They were on foot and under his personal command. The purpose of the army was to capture his brother, Duke Senior, and put him to the sword and kill him. Duke Frederick came to the outskirts of this forest, where he met an old religious man. After some conversation with him, Duke Frederick was converted both from his attempt to kill his brother and from this world. He has bequeathed his crown to his banished brother, and he has restored all their lands to those who were exiled with his banished brother. On my life, I swear that this is true."

Duke Senior said, "Welcome, young man. You have brought handsome gifts to your brothers' weddings. Oliver will get the land of his late father, and Orlando, who is marrying my only child, Rosalind, will get my powerful Dukedom after I die."

He added, "Now, in this forest, let us perform the four weddings that here were well begun and well conceived. Afterward, all of this happy number who have endured difficult days and nights with us shall share the good of our returned fortune, according to their ranks. In the meantime, let us forget this newly acquired courtly honor and enjoy our rustic revelry. Play, musicians! And you, brides and bridegrooms all, with your happiness overflowing its cup, dance."

"Jaques de Boys, sir, just a moment," Jaques said. "If I heard you rightly, Duke Frederick will now lead a religious life as a monk and has cast away life in the glamorous court?"

"That is true," Jaques de Boys replied.

"I will go to him," Jaques said. "He has converted to a religious life, and from converts such as him there is much to be heard and learned."

Jaques said to Duke Senior, "To you I leave your former rank; because of your patience and your virtue, you well deserve it."

Jaques said to Orlando, "To you I leave a love that your true faith truly deserves."

Jaques said to Oliver, "To you I leave your land and love and great allies at the court."

Jaques said to Silvius, "To you I leave a long and well-deserved sex life."

Jaques said to Touchstone, "To you I leave marital argument because the loving part of your marriage will last about two months."

To everyone, Jaques said, "So, enjoy your pleasures. I am for other than for dancing measures. I am melancholy, and I do not dance."

"Stay, Jaques, stay," Duke Senior said.

"I am not the man to enjoy a celebration," Jaques said. "I will stay at your soon-to-be-abandoned cave to hear later whatever you want to say to me."

Jaques left.

Duke Senior said to everyone, "Proceed, proceed. We will begin these marriage rites the same way that we hope that they will end: in true delights."

They danced and celebrated.

EPILOGUE

The author of this book now whisks you, the reader, back to the year 1600 or so, when Shakespeare was still alive, and when male actors performed the roles of all women in plays.

A young man who has just finished performing the role of Rosalind in *As You Like It* now steps in front of the theatrical curtain and says, "It is not the fashion to see the lady recite the epilogue, but it is no more unbecoming than to see the Lord recite the prologue. If it is true that good wine needs no advertising, then it is true that a good play needs no epilogue. Nevertheless, good wine is advertised, and good plays are made better with the help of good epilogues.

"But I am in a strange position. I do not have a good epilogue, and I cannot ingratiate myself with you in the behalf of a good play!

"I am not costumed like a beggar; therefore, begging will not become me. Instead, I will bewitch you and cast a spell on you.

"I will begin with the women. I command you, women, because you love men, to like as much of this play as pleases you.

"And I command you, men, because you love women — and I see by your smiles that none of you hates women — that between you and the women this play may please.

"If I were a woman, I would kiss as many of you men as had beards that pleased me, complexions that I liked, and breaths that were not foul.

"I am sure that the many men who have good beards or good faces or sweet breaths will, for the kind offer I have made, applaud to bid me farewell when I curtsey."

The male actor curtsies and exits to great applause.

APPENDIX A: ABOUT THE AUTHOR

It was a dark and stormy night. Suddenly a cry rang out, and on a hot summer night in 1954, Josephine, wife of Carl Bruce, gave birth to a boy — me. Unfortunately, this young married couple allowed Reuben Saturday, Josephine's brother, to name their first-born. Reuben, aka "The Joker," decided that Bruce was a nice name, so he decided to name me Bruce Bruce. I have gone by my middle name — David — ever since.

Being named Bruce David Bruce hasn't been all bad. Bank tellers remember me very quickly, so I don't often have to show an ID. It can be fun in charades, also. When I was a counselor as a teenager at Camp Echoing Hills in Warsaw, Ohio, a fellow counselor gave the signs for "sounds like" and "two words," then she pointed to a bruise on her leg twice. Bruise Bruise? Oh yeah, Bruce Bruce is the answer!

Uncle Reuben, by the way, gave me a haircut when I was in kindergarten. He cut my hair short and shaved a small bald spot on the back of my head. My mother wouldn't let me go to school until the bald spot grew out again.

Of all my brothers and sisters (six in all), I am the only transplant to Athens, Ohio. I was born in Newark, Ohio, and have lived all around Southeastern Ohio. However, I moved to Athens to go to Ohio University and have never left.

At Ohio U, I never could make up my mind whether to major in English or Philosophy, so I got a bachelor's degree with a double major in both areas, then I added a Master's of Arts degree in English and a Master's of Arts degree in Philosophy. Yes, I have my MAMA degree.

Currently, and for a long time to come (I eat fruits and veggies), I am spending my retirement writing books such as *Nadia Comaneci: Perfect 10*, *The Funniest People in Dance*, *Homer's* Iliad: *A Retelling in Prose*, and *William Shakespeare's* Othello: *A Retelling in Prose.*

By the way, my sister Brenda Kennedy writes romances such as *A New Beginning* and *Shattered Dreams*.

APPENDIX B: SOME BOOKS BY DAVID BRUCE

Retellings of a Classic Work of Literature

Arden of Faversham*: A Retelling*

Ben Jonson's The Alchemist: *A Retelling*

Ben Jonson's The Arraignment, or Poetaster: *A Retelling*

Ben Jonson's Bartholomew Fair: *A Retelling*

Ben Jonson's The Case is Altered: *A Retelling*

Ben Jonson's Catiline's Conspiracy: *A Retelling*

Ben Jonson's The Devil is an Ass: *A Retelling*

Ben Jonson's Epicene: *A Retelling*

Ben Jonson's Every Man in His Humor: *A Retelling*

Ben Jonson's Every Man Out of His Humor: *A Retelling*

Ben Jonson's The Fountain of Self-Love, or Cynthia's Revels: *A Retelling*

Ben Jonson's The Magnetic Lady, or Humors Reconciled: *A Retelling*

Ben Jonson's The New Inn, or The Light Heart: *A Retelling*

Ben Jonson's Sejanus' Fall: *A Retelling*

Ben Jonson's The Staple of News: *A Retelling*

Ben Jonson's A Tale of a Tub: *A Retelling*

Ben Jonson's Volpone, or the Fox: *A Retelling*

Christopher Marlowe's Complete Plays: Retellings

Christopher Marlowe's Dido, Queen of Carthage: *A Retelling*

Christopher Marlowe's Doctor Faustus: *Retellings of the 1604 A-Text and of the 1616 B-Text*

Christopher Marlowe's Edward II: *A Retelling*

Christopher Marlowe's The Massacre at Paris: *A Retelling*

Christopher Marlowe's The Rich Jew of Malta: *A Retelling*

Christopher Marlowe's Tamburlaine, Parts 1 and 2: *Retellings*

Dante's Divine Comedy: *A Retelling in Prose*

Dante's Inferno: *A Retelling in Prose*

Dante's Purgatory: *A Retelling in Prose*

Dante's Paradise: *A Retelling in Prose*

The Famous Victories of Henry V: *A Retelling*

From the Iliad *to the* Odyssey*: A Retelling in Prose of Quintus of Smyrna's* Posthomerica

George Chapman, Ben Jonson, and John Marston's Eastward Ho! *A Retelling*

George Peele's The Arraignment of Paris: *A Retelling*

George Peele's The Battle of Alcazar: *A Retelling*

George's Peele's David and Bathsheba, and the Tragedy of Absalom: *A Retelling*

George Peele's Edward I: *A Retelling*

George Peele's The Old Wives' Tale: *A Retelling*

George-a-Greene: *A Retelling*
The History of King Leir: *A Retelling*
Homer's Iliad: *A Retelling in Prose*
Homer's Odyssey: *A Retelling in Prose*
J.W. Gent.'s The Valiant Scot: *A Retelling*
Jason and the Argonauts: A Retelling in Prose of Apollonius of Rhodes' Argonautica
John Ford: Eight Plays Translated into Modern English
John Ford's The Broken Heart: *A Retelling*
John Ford's The Fancies, Chaste and Noble: *A Retelling*
John Ford's The Lady's Trial: *A Retelling*
John Ford's The Lover's Melancholy: *A Retelling*
John Ford's Love's Sacrifice: *A Retelling*
John Ford's Perkin Warbeck: *A Retelling*
John Ford's The Queen: *A Retelling*
John Ford's 'Tis Pity She's a Whore: *A Retelling*
John Lyly's Campaspe: *A Retelling*
John Lyly's Endymion, The Man in the Moon: *A Retelling*
John Lyly's Galatea: *A Retelling*
John Lyly's Love's Metamorphosis: *A Retelling*
John Lyly's Midas: *A Retelling*
John Lyly's Mother Bombie: *A Retelling*
John Lyly's Sappho and Phao: *A Retelling*
John Lyly's The Woman in the Moon: *A Retelling*
John Webster's The White Devil: *A Retelling*
King Edward III: *A Retelling*
Mankind: *A Medieval Morality Play* (A Retelling)
Margaret Cavendish's The Unnatural Tragedy: *A Retelling*
The Merry Devil of Edmonton: *A Retelling*
The Summoning of Everyman: *A Medieval Morality Play* (A Retelling)
Robert Greene's Friar Bacon and Friar Bungay: *A Retelling*
The Taming of a Shrew: *A Retelling*
Tarlton's Jests: A Retelling
Thomas Middleton's A Chaste Maid in Cheapside: *A Retelling*
Thomas Middleton's Women Beware Women: *A Retelling*
Thomas Middleton and Thomas Dekker's The Roaring Girl: *A Retelling*
Thomas Middleton and William Rowley's The Changeling: *A Retelling*
The Trojan War and Its Aftermath: Four Ancient Epic Poems
Virgil's Aeneid: *A Retelling in Prose*
William Shakespeare's 5 Late Romances: Retellings in Prose
William Shakespeare's 10 Histories: Retellings in Prose
William Shakespeare's 11 Tragedies: Retellings in Prose
William Shakespeare's 12 Comedies: Retellings in Prose

William Shakespeare's 38 Plays: Retellings in Prose
William Shakespeare's 1 Henry IV, aka Henry IV, Part 1: *A Retelling in Prose*
William Shakespeare's 2 Henry IV, aka Henry IV, Part 2: *A Retelling in Prose*
William Shakespeare's 1 Henry VI, aka Henry VI, Part 1: *A Retelling in Prose*
William Shakespeare's 2 Henry VI, aka Henry VI, Part 2: *A Retelling in Prose*
William Shakespeare's 3 Henry VI, aka Henry VI, Part 3: *A Retelling in Prose*
William Shakespeare's All's Well that Ends Well: *A Retelling in Prose*
William Shakespeare's Antony and Cleopatra: *A Retelling in Prose*
William Shakespeare's As You Like It: *A Retelling in Prose*
William Shakespeare's The Comedy of Errors: *A Retelling in Prose*
William Shakespeare's Coriolanus: *A Retelling in Prose*
William Shakespeare's Cymbeline: *A Retelling in Prose*
William Shakespeare's Hamlet: *A Retelling in Prose*
William Shakespeare's Henry V: *A Retelling in Prose*
William Shakespeare's Henry VIII: *A Retelling in Prose*
William Shakespeare's Julius Caesar: *A Retelling in Prose*
William Shakespeare's King John: *A Retelling in Prose*
William Shakespeare's King Lear: *A Retelling in Prose*
William Shakespeare's Love's Labor's Lost: *A Retelling in Prose*
William Shakespeare's Macbeth: *A Retelling in Prose*
William Shakespeare's Measure for Measure: *A Retelling in Prose*
William Shakespeare's The Merchant of Venice: *A Retelling in Prose*
William Shakespeare's The Merry Wives of Windsor: *A Retelling in Prose*
William Shakespeare's A Midsummer Night's Dream: *A Retelling in Prose*
William Shakespeare's Much Ado About Nothing: *A Retelling in Prose*
William Shakespeare's Othello: *A Retelling in Prose*
William Shakespeare's Pericles, Prince of Tyre: *A Retelling in Prose*
William Shakespeare's Richard II: *A Retelling in Prose*
William Shakespeare's Richard III: *A Retelling in Prose*
William Shakespeare's Romeo and Juliet: *A Retelling in Prose*
William Shakespeare's The Taming of the Shrew: *A Retelling in Prose*
William Shakespeare's The Tempest: *A Retelling in Prose*
William Shakespeare's Timon of Athens: *A Retelling in Prose*
William Shakespeare's Titus Andronicus: *A Retelling in Prose*
William Shakespeare's Troilus and Cressida: *A Retelling in Prose*
William Shakespeare's Twelfth Night: *A Retelling in Prose*
William Shakespeare's The Two Gentlemen of Verona: *A Retelling in Prose*
William Shakespeare's The Two Noble Kinsmen: *A Retelling in Prose*
William Shakespeare's The Winter's Tale: *A Retelling in Prose*

Printed by Libri Plureos GmbH in Hamburg,
Germany